From the minute the new nanny had set foot in the house, she'd brought Pierce nothing but complications

He didn't understand Nicole; he didn't know how to deal with her. She turned his orderly life upside down and usurped his authority.... Yet despite all that, the fact remained: he enjoyed every minute of the aggravation she brought to his life.

He found himself watching her as she interacted with Tom. He was blown away by her patience and tenderness with the little boy. And he'd even gone so far as to wonder how she'd be with a child of her own, a baby. *His* baby....

Dear Reader,

A perfect nanny can be tough to find, but once you've found her you'll love and treasure her forever. She's someone who'll not only look after the kids but could also be that loving mom they never knew. Or sometimes she's a he and is the daddy they aspire to.

Here at Harlequin Presents we've put together a compelling new series, NANNY WANTED!, in which some of our most popular authors create nannies whose talents extend way beyond taking care of the children! Each story will excite and delight you and make you wonder how any family could be complete without a nineties nanny.

Remember—nanny knows best when it comes to falling in love!

The Editors

Look out next month for:

The Millionaire's Baby by Diana Hamilton (#1956)

CATHERINE SPENCER

A Nanny in the Family

Harlequin Books

TORONTO • NEW YORK • LONDON
AMSTERDAM • PARIS • SYDNEY • HAMBURG
STOCKHOLM • ATHENS • TOKYO • MILAN
MADRID • WARSAW • BUDAPEST • AUCKLAND

ISBN 0-373-11950-X

A NANNY IN THE FAMILY

First North American Publication 1998.

Copyright © 1997 by Kathy Garner.

This edition published by arrangement with Harlequin Books S.A.

® and TM are trademarks of the publisher. Trademarks indicated with ® are registered in the United States Patent and Trademark Office, the Canadian Trade Marks Office and in other countries.

Printed in U.S.A.

CHAPTER ONE

IT SHOULD have been raining, with the drops falling from the trees softly, steadily, like the tears she'd shed all night long. The sky should have been draped in mourning gray and the ocean swathed in funeral mist. Instead, the day was indecently gorgeous, with the sun beating down and the gardens flaming with geraniums and early roses.

Even the house seemed to smile, with its mellow rosy pink walls and sparkling paned windows. Four elegant chimneys posed against the clear sky, the white painted woodwork gleamed, the brass door knocker shone brilliantly. Or was it the threat of yet more tears blinding her so thoroughly that she had to blink repeatedly before she dared step out of the car?

Suddenly, the front door swung open and a middle-aged woman appeared. She paused on the top step and spoke to someone standing out of sight within the house. Shook her head commiseratingly and reached one hand forward as though to pat the unseen person's arm.

She looked, Nicole thought, exactly the way a nanny should look: pleasingly plump, competent and cheerful in her print dress and sensible white shoes. The last thing Tommy needed at this point in his life was a woman drearily mired in her own misery.

Blinking again, Nicole swung her gaze away and stared at a bed of deep blue hydrangeas flanked by spiny white Shasta daisies the size of baseballs. *Be here at two*, the voice on the phone had said, and it had been exactly five minutes to the hour when she'd turned off the quiet road and driven through the wrought iron gates described by the woman she'd met yesterday, at Arlene's

5

house. She had a minute, two at the most, in which to prepare herself for the most consummate performance of her life. Yet how did a person push aside a grief so new, even for a moment? Worse, how to keep it permanently in the background, hidden under a facade of serene capability?

The other applicant came down the steps, large white handbag slung over her sturdy wrist. She nodded pleasantly as she passed Nicole's car and continued down the drive, planting one foot solidly in front of the other.

She would be kind and firm. Under her care, Tommy would learn to like green beans and spinach, and go to bed on time. When he cried for his mommy and daddy, he would be taken up on that ample lap and comforted. But it wouldn't be enough. Only she, Nicole, could truly understand his loss, and only she could compensate for it.

The front door to the house stood open still and another woman, older and more slender than the first, beckoned to her from the top step. Nicole nodded and glanced quickly in her rearview mirror, thankful to see the eyedrops she'd used had reduced the redness brought on by a night of weeping. She could not afford to look distraught. She dare not break down.

"You must be the young lady who phoned just this morning. Miss Bennett, right?" The woman at the door spoke with a trace of a British accent and wore a starched white apron over her plain gray dress. "It's good that you're on time. The Commander expects punctuality."

The Commander expects. The words filled Nicole with dread, evoking an image of aging but erect military bearing born of regimented discipline. And Tommy was only four. Oh, the poor baby!

"Have there been many other applicants for the job?" she asked, quickly before she burst into tears again.

"Only three, I'm afraid." The woman shook her head. "You're our last hope unless someone else turns up unexpectedly. Commander Warner's at his wit's end, what with losing his cousin so tragically and then, with poor Doctor Jim and his wife barely cold in their graves, finding himself standing in as Daddy for their boy.''

She pulled a tissue from her apron pocket and wiped at the tears filming her eyes.

Don't cry, Nicole silently begged, *or you'll start me off again and I'm afraid I'll never stop.* ''I take it,'' she said, ''that Commander Warner has no children of his own?''

''Gracious, no,'' the woman exclaimed, recovering herself. ''He's not even married—though not from want of trying on some people's part! The most he's been used to is playing long-distance uncle to young Tommy. Not that he's the boy's uncle exactly—second cousin, more like—but what does it matter? The important thing is, they've got each other and thank God for it, or I don't know how either of them would get through this dreadful time. Come along this way, dear. The Commander's interviewing in the library.''

A long hall with a dark polished wood floor covered by a carpet runner stretched from the front door to the rear of the house. Following behind the woman, Nicole passed a wide archway leading into a formal living room flooded with sunlight.

Directly opposite, a similar archway showed a dining room with a Duncan Phyfe table and eight high-backed chairs set precisely in the middle of a pale Aubusson rug. Was that where Tommy took his meals now, and did the Commander realize that four-year-olds occasionally spilled food on the floor?

''Miss Bennett's here, Commander.''

''Thank you, Janet. Show her in.'' His voice was deep and smoothly rich, a crooner's voice almost, ludicrously at odds with the authoritarian impression Nicole had built of him.

The woman smiled encouragingly at Nicole, then turned away down another, narrower hall that led under the curving staircase to what was probably the kitchen wing.

Don't leave me, Nicole wanted to call after her. *I can't handle this alone!*

"Are you there, Miss Bennett?" The voice from the library rang with an edge of impatience this time, suggesting there was steel under all that velvet.

"Yes," she said, still from beyond the threshold of the room.

"Then be so good as to present yourself in the flesh."

There was no mistaking the steel now. Any more shilly-shallying on her part and the interview would be concluded before it had begun. Bracing herself, she walked into the library with what she prayed would strike exactly the proper blend of ability and deference such an old curmudgeon would undoubtedly expect of an underling.

The man rising from behind a handsome Georgian desk to shake her hand, however, looked anything but the part she'd assigned to him. Mid-thirtyish, tall and broad-shouldered, with devastatingly blue eyes and a granite jaw, he epitomized vintage Hollywood at its most alluring.

At any other time, Nicole might have dwelled on the romantic potential of such a fine specimen. As things stood now, however, he was merely the means to an end and could have two heads, for all she cared.

"How do you do? I'm Pierce Warner." His handclasp was brief and firm. "Please be seated, Miss Bennett."

"Thank you," she replied, appalled to hear her words hanging in the air, breathy as a teenager's.

The last time she'd been this nervous was when she'd appeared for her final interview at The Clinic. The ink on her nursing degree had been barely dry at the time and if she'd been asked how many limbs the human body normally came equipped with, she'd probably have given the wrong answer. But that was six years ago and she'd have thought herself past the sort of uncertainty that gripped her now.

She'd nursed terminally ill children, she'd comforted bereaved parents, and even though she'd many times thought her own heart would break for them all, she'd somehow managed to control her emotions. So why was she falling apart now, at this most crucial time?

"Tell me about yourself, Miss Bennett," the Commander commanded, fixing her in the sort of close scrutiny that missed nothing.

"Well," she began, discreetly wiping damp palms on her skirt, "I'm new to the area."

Dark eyebrows raised disparagingly, he said, "That strikes you as relevant, does it?"

"Yes—um, no!" She stopped and blew out a small breath. "What I mean is, I expect you'd like to speak to my previous employers, but I recently moved to the west coast, so I'm afraid I can't offer you any local names. But I do have good references."

She reached into the straw bag on her lap, withdrew the manila envelope containing her credentials, and offered it to him.

He set it aside and folded his hands on the desk. His fingernails, she noted, were short and scrupulously clean. "At this point," he said, subjecting her to another all-encompassing stare, "I'm more interested in hearing why *you* think you're the best person to fill the position of nanny to my ward."

She expelled another long breath, hoping that the next time she opened her mouth, she'd make a better impression. Once again, though, she said exactly the wrong thing. "Well, I'd better explain right off that I've never been a nanny before."

His gaze narrowed as if he'd just sighted an enemy vessel heaving over the horizon. "Now *that* strikes me as decidedly relevant. Would you care to explain why you're bothering to waste both my time and yours?"

"Because," she said, plunging in and praying she'd

remember the lines she'd rehearsed all through last night, "I am very experienced in dealing with children, particularly those under stress. And I'm aware that your... ward—" The cold Victorian description stuck in her throat, nearly choking her. This was Tommy they were talking about. Her nephew. A warm, living child desperately in need of the love and comfort she was so willing to give to him.

"Go on, Miss Bennett."

Could he see the way she was twisting her hands together in her lap? Did he guess that her skin was clammy with cold, even though the temperature outside hovered near eighty? "I'm aware," she said, closing her mind to everything but the need to convince him that she was exactly the person he was looking for, "that your family has recently faced a terrible tragedy as a result of which your ward lost both his parents. Allow me to offer you my deepest sympathy."

He inclined his head in a gesture of acknowledgment, a cool, almost detached response, one might have thought, had not the sudden twitch of muscle in his jaw betrayed emotions being kept rigidly in check.

"I have taken an extended leave of absence from my previous job and come to Oregon to be near my relatives," she went on, veering as close to the truth as she dared. "However, I do need to support myself, and I thought, when I heard you were looking for a full-time nanny, that it was a position I could very well fill."

She leaned forward, her confidence spurred by the recitation of facts which were not cloaked in lies. "I'm a pediatric nurse, Commander Warner. For the past three years I've worked exclusively in the intensive care unit of my hospital. ICU nurses receive a great deal of exposure to death. They learn to deal with it compassionately. If they don't, they don't last long. I can help your ward through this difficult time and I'm available to start looking after him immediately."

For the first time, the Commander looked marginally impressed. "How old are you?" he asked.

"Twenty-nine."

He flexed his fingers and rapped a soft tattoo on the desk surface. "Tommy's mother just turned twenty-eight," he said, staring bleakly out of the window beside him.

I know, Nicole could have told him. *She was eighteen months younger than I. Her birthday was in February.* Instead, she said, "I think having him cared for by someone close to his mother's age might help."

"I agree." He pulled the manila envelope closer and set it on the blotter in front of him. "You realize this is a live-in position? That you won't have much spare time to spend with your relatives? I'd need you here at least five days a week."

Relief almost made her careless. It was all she could do not to tell him that she'd prefer to work around the clock, seven days a week. "Of course."

"Your sleep might be disturbed at times. Tom has cried every night for his mother."

Oh, darling! she thought, her arms aching to hold the child almost as badly as her heart broke for him. She swallowed and said briskly, "I'm a nurse. Shift work is second nature to me."

He whistled tunelessly under his breath a moment, then slewed another glance her way. "The response to my ad has been disappointing. The woman I saw this morning wasn't much more than a child herself and totally unsuitable. The one who was here before you has spent the last eleven years with the same family and would have been ideal for the job, but she isn't free to start working for me until the end of the month."

Nicole held her breath, sensing victory within her grasp. As if to clinch the matter, from somewhere within the house a child's cry broke the silence.

"I don't think I can wait that long," the Commander decided, and touched the tip of the envelope with his forefinger. "These references...I suppose I should read them. Or are they just the usual claptrap?"

"That's something only you can decide."

"Right." He shrugged. "Would you like some coffee or a cold drink, Miss Bennett?"

"A glass of water would be nice."

His slow smile creased his cheeks with unexpected dimples. "I think we can do better than that," he said, indicating the open French doors on the other side of the room. "I'll have Janet bring something to you on the patio."

The view outside stole Nicole's breath away. Perched on a bluff, the house flowed down to the beach in a series of terraces connected by brick-paved paths. A curved flight of steps similar to those at the front door gave way to a swimming pool set in a natural rock depression. To either side, flower beds edged an expanse of closely trimmed lawn. Below, the great spread of the ocean reflected the cloudless blue sky.

From a walkway covered by a vine-draped pergola, Janet appeared, a loaded tray in her hands. "Lovely sight, isn't it?" she remarked, setting the tray on an umbrella-shaded table and coming to stand beside Nicole. "A body can just feel the peace soaking into her bones."

Nicole couldn't. Her entire body was suffused with pain. God might seem to be in His heaven but, appearances to the contrary, things were far from right in her world. The beauty and tranquillity were an affront.

Janet turned away to pour liquid from a frosty pitcher into a tall, stemmed glass. "How did the interview go?"

"I'm not sure. I hope I get the job."

"Well, dear, I can tell you the Commander won't bother keeping anyone around who doesn't measure up. If he thought he was wasting his time with you, you'd be out the door by now. Try this lemonade. It's the real thing, made from scratch."

"Thank you."

"And here's a plate of biscuits—cookies, you call them—if you'd like something to eat while you wait."

Breakfast was a distant memory and dinner last night nonexistent, but the thought of food nauseated Nicole. Still, out of politeness, she nibbled at one of the cookies and said, "What I'd really like is to meet the little boy. Could you bring him out to see me, do you think?"

She'd said the wrong thing again. Janet backed off as if she'd been indecently propositioned.

"Oh, it's not up to me to allow that, dear!" she exclaimed, her accent broadened by shock. "That's something for the Commander to allow if he decides you're best for the job."

But he's my nephew and I need to see him, Nicole thought. I need to hold him, to smell the little boy scent of his hair, to kiss the soft sweet skin of his neck. I need to know that he doesn't feel alone and abandoned.

Janet straightened the bib of her apron and sighed. "I just hope he makes up his mind quickly. I don't mind telling you, I've got my hands full trying to run the house and keep tabs on Tommy at the same time. He's a good little boy, but at that age, you know, a child is only ever still when he's asleep."

"Where is he now?"

"Taking a nap. He does that most afternoons for about half an hour." Janet touched Nicole's arm sympathetically. "I'm sure the Commander will bring him down and introduce you, if he likes what he's being told about you."

"Being told?"

Janet leaned forward confidingly. "He was on the phone long distance when I took in his lemonade, and I just happened to overhear your name being mentioned."

Exhaustion and stress must be catching up with her, Nicole decided, stifling an untoward giggle at the thought of The Commander sipping lemonade. Wouldn't a tot of rum be more his style? "Why do you call him the Commander?"

"That's his rank. He's a Navy man, didn't you know? Works designing warships now, of course, on account of his bad back and all, but it was a dreadful disappointment to him that he couldn't remain on active service. He knew he wanted to go to sea from the time he was Tommy's age. Learned to sail a dinghy before he turned eight and spent every spare minute hanging around the yacht basin. Knew the name and make of every boat there, built models of most of them, too. Then, as soon as he was old enough, he was off to the Naval Academy and after that, it was glory all the way. Quite the local hero, you might say."

She leaned close again, as though what she was about to impart was a well guarded secret revealed only to a chosen few. "You should see all his medals. He was in the Gulf War, you know—that's when he was injured, rescuing one of his men in an explosion on the bridge—and decorated for bravery, or however they call it."

"Why don't you tell her my shoe size while you're at it, Janet?" the object of all this admiration remarked, strolling out through the French doors and smiling at the housekeeper. His eyes, Nicole thought, were even bluer than the sky and his smile dazzling.

"Oh, Commander!" Janet exclaimed, blushing like a girl. "I didn't hear you come out."

"So I gather." Sobering, he switched his gaze to Nicole. "Bring your lemonade inside and let's talk some more, Miss Bennett."

Did he ever say "please" or "thank you," or was he so used to dishing out orders that it never occurred to him to remember his manners?

"Why didn't you tell me you'd worked at The Mayo Clinic?" he began, as soon as they were seated across the desk from each other again.

She couldn't help herself. The question was out before she could stop it. "That strikes you as relevant, does it?"

He didn't exactly smile at her impudence, but his eyes

glimmered with amusement. "If you were in the Navy, Miss Bennett, I'd reprimand you for rank insubordination. As it is, I have to wonder what it is about this job that appeals to you. You must know you're seriously overqualified for the position I'm trying to fill."

"On paper, perhaps," she said, "but I need a change."

"How so?"

Once again grief threatened to rise up and engulf her. To buy herself enough time to regain control, she paced to the French doors and stood with her back to him so that he couldn't see the sudden shine of tears in her eyes. "Any nurse working in a critical care unit will tell you that professional burnout is common," she said, fighting to subdue the quiver in her voice. "You might think we become inured to death, but we don't. And when those touched by it are children, the stress factor is particularly severe."

She paused, hating the fact that she was about to add another lie to those she'd already told him. Deceit did not come easily and she wished she dared tell him the whole truth. But it was too soon. The risks were too great. "I felt it was time for me to take a break."

"I appreciate that, Miss Bennett, and I sympathize. But my first priority is my ward's welfare and I wonder how ably you will meet his needs feeling as you do. He needs a great deal of emotional support right now. How well do you think you can supply that, considering your own admittedly fragile state?"

"Just because I feel the need for a change doesn't alter the fact that I love children," she said, thankful to be on completely honest ground again. "And you may depend on me always to put your ward's interests ahead of my own."

"I shall hold you to that."

She dared to look at him again then, hope surging within her breast. "Are you telling me I have the job?"

"Not quite. Before we make that decision, I think you must meet Tom."

Yes! "That would be sensible," she said soberly. "No point in reaching any decisions until we see how we get along."

As if there was any doubt that she wouldn't adore him on sight!

"I'll get him," the Commander said, stuffing her résumé and references back into the envelope and handing it to her. "He might be a bit shy with you—he's seen a lot of strangers in the last week and is obviously confused—but I'm sure you'll allow for that."

"Of course."

He was gone for several minutes. Aware of the slender hold she had on her emotions, and knowing that the Commander would pick up on any false move, Nicole spent the interval schooling herself to composure. She had just this one last hurdle to clear. No matter what it cost her, she must present a calm and reassuring front if she wanted to convince him beyond any doubt that she was the best possible nanny for Tommy.

She thought she had succeeded. She thought that all the years of working in ICU would stand her in good stead. This, after all, was a healthy little child, not some poor, sickly soul with no future. But when the door opened and she saw the boy in the Commander's arms, she forgot everything: her training, her rehearsing, her lies. Everything.

"This is Tom, Miss Bennett."

Instead of saying something rational like, "Hello, Tommy, it's nice to meet you," Nicole pressed her fingers to her mouth to stop its trembling and whispered, "Oh! Oh, I knew he would be beautiful, but I had no idea he'd be so completely perfect!"

"Wait until he's woken you up at five in the morning three days in a row, before you decide that," the Commander said dryly, swinging Tommy to the floor.

The child staggered a little against his uncle's knee

and regarded Nicole from big solemn eyes. His face was flushed with sleep and his hair damp on one side from perspiration. A worn baby quilt trailed from one dimpled hand.

The need to hold him, to press his sweetly rounded little body close to her heart, left Nicole aching. But she dared not gratify that need; the tears simmered too close to the surface, threatening to gush forth and destroy the image she'd struggled so hard to present. Instead she turned aside, quickly, before the spasm contorting her features gave her away, rummaged blindly in her bag for a tissue, and dabbed at her nose.

"Forgive me," she said, praying the Commander hadn't noticed anything amiss. "I thought I felt a sneeze coming on but it changed its mind."

"You have a cold, perhaps?"

"No," she hastened to assure him. "I'm as healthy as the proverbial horse." Then before she gave rise to any other suspicions, she squatted down and drummed up a smile for Tommy. "Hi, sweetheart. I'm Nicole."

"Hi," he said, and she thought that if angels spoke, they would sound just as he did.

"That's a really nice quilt you've got. Do you take it to bed with you?"

"Yes," he said, detaching himself from his uncle's leg and advancing a step or two closer to her. "It's my dee-dee."

"It's a blanket, Tom," the Commander said, kindly enough. "Big boys don't use baby talk. Let me see you shake hands with Miss Bennett."

Heavenly days, the man had no more idea how to speak to a four-year-old than she had to an orangutan! "Why don't you show me the garden, instead?" she said, sensing the child's discomfort with the adult behavior expected of him. "If your uncle doesn't mind...?"

Somewhat after the fact, she glanced at the Commander. "Not at all," he said. "It will give you a chance to become better acquainted. Go ahead and show Miss Bennett the garden, Tom.''

''All right.'' Tommy perked up. ''But not the pool. I'm not allowed to go to the pool by myself. It's against the rules.''

''Not the pool,'' Nicole agreed. ''I'd rather see the flowers, instead.''

He considered her for a moment, then came forward and took her hand. ''I have a garden at home,'' he told her chattily. ''I planted seeds in it and watered them.''

''Did you?'' she said, enchanted by him.

''Yes. And they grew as big as a tree.'' He gestured grandly, his face alive with excitement.

''Now, Tom!'' his ''uncle'' warned. ''Remember we talked about exaggerating? Stick to the facts, please.''

Truly, she would need to tape her mouth shut if this was the man's idea of dealing with a child of four! Swallowing the objections fairly itching to make themselves heard, Nicole gave Tommy's hand a reassuring squeeze.

It didn't console him. ''I'm just teasing,'' he said, the animation in his face seeping away and his lip trembling ominously. ''Mommy laughs when I tease her. I want to see my mommy. Can I go home now?''

''He keeps asking me that,'' the Commander muttered, a flash of panic sparking in his blue eyes, ''and I don't know quite what to tell him.''

''Since you're so anxious to stick to the facts, perhaps you should tell him the truth,'' she said, then turned again to her nephew. ''You're living here now, darling, but we can go and see your house sometime, if you like.''

''Will Mommy be there?'' he asked, the question enough to bring the lump back to Nicole's throat, bigger than ever.

''No, Tommy. But perhaps we can find a picture of her.''

"Oh." He fingered the quilt again. "And one of Daddy, as well, right?"

"Yes, darling."

He tilted his head and smiled at her. "The flowers are red," he said.

Grateful beyond words that he'd chosen to change the subject before she collapsed in yet another soggy heap of tears, Nicole said teasingly, "What, all of them?"

"And yellow and purple." He tugged on her hand. "And pink and black and purple."

"Black?" she echoed, allowing him to lead her out of the French doors and into the sunlight. "I don't think I've ever seen black flowers before. Show them to me."

"There are no black flowers, Tom," the Commander chastised. "You mustn't tell untruths."

Oh, please! Nicole rolled her eyes and wondered if the man had any memory at all of being young and full of wonder at a world whose magic was limited only by the scope of imagination.

"Purple," Tommy said obligingly. "Very purple. I prefer purple flowers."

"You *prefer*?" Nicole laughed for what seemed the first time in years.

"He uses some very adult words at times," the Commander said. "Then, for no reason, he suddenly reverts to baby talk which I must admit I find annoying."

You would, she thought. You'd *prefer* him to take a giant leap from infancy to adulthood, with nothing in between to cushion the transition. "They all do, Commander, at this age. It's not uncommon and he'll stop a lot sooner if we don't make a big deal about it."

"You might be right, I suppose."

"I am right," she assured him. "Trust me, I've handled enough four-year-olds to know."

He inclined his head in what she supposed was agreement and removed a key from a ring he withdrew from his pocket. "I'll leave the two of you to become better acquainted. If you'd like to go down to the beach, there are steps at the end of the property but you'll need this to get through the gate. Please be sure you lock it behind you when you come back. I don't want the boy going down there unsupervised. The tides are treacherous.''

He stood on the patio and watched them a moment or two then turned back to the house at the sound of a woman's voice, too silvery to be Janet's, calling his name. Nicole heard the deep rumble of his response and a waterfall of feminine laughter drift out on the still air. Who was the visitor? she wondered. The woman in his life?

She hoped so. The more he was occupied with other affairs, the less time he would have to interfere in her relationship with Tommy.

She looked down at the child by her side and felt her heart swell with love. He was blond and blue-eyed, like his mother. His skin was soft and fine, his cheeks pink, his sturdy little legs slightly suntanned.

Nicole wanted to hug him fiercely to her, to kiss him and tell him that she loved him, but reminded herself that although she knew everything about him, he knew nothing of her. Such a display of affection would make him uneasy and the last thing she wanted was for the Commander to pick up on that and decide she wasn't suited to the job, after all.

They came to the gate, set in a brick wall at the cliff's edge. There were a hundred and eighty-eight steps leading down the other side, winding under trees bent by winter gales into weird and wonderful shapes, and protected on each side by a split cedar railing.

When they reached the bottom, Tommy tugged his hand free and raced away from her across the sand, sheer exuberance in every line of his perfect little body.

"I will take care of him, Arlene," Nicole whispered, never taking her eyes off him. "You and I were robbed of twenty-five years of knowing we were sisters but I will make sure your son never forgets you. Your baby will be safe with me.''

It was the most sacred promise she'd ever made, one she'd hold to no matter what the cost.

CHAPTER TWO

"WELL, you've finally come back!"

Still blinded by the sun's glare, it took Nicole a moment or two to discern the owner of the amused voice that greeted her when she and Tommy returned to the library.

She squinted at the figure reclining in one of two leather wing chairs beside a fireplace heaped with dried peony blossoms. "Were we gone very long?"

"Pierce is about ready to call out the National Guard." The woman was elegantly thin and quite startlingly beautiful. "Being thrust into instant fatherhood has made him very nervous. He's afraid you've kidnapped the boy."

"I'm sorry if I worried you."

"Oh, you didn't worry me," the woman assured her. "But Pierce is taking his guardianship responsibilities very seriously and seems to feel he has to be on patrol twenty-four hours a day. Are you going to take the job?"

"If it's offered to me, yes."

"I'm sure it will be." The woman ran a speculative hazel gaze over Nicole, from her head to her toes and back again. "You certainly have my vote."

"Thank you."

"My pleasure. You've got that look of durability about you that the job requires, although you do dress somewhat more stylishly than I'd have thought suitable." She yawned delicately. "Better you than me, is all I can say."

"You don't care for children?" Nicole asked, feeling a bit like a Clydesdale horse being assessed for working stamina.

"Of course I do—at a distance. But I certainly don't want them planting their sticky little paws all over my good clothes. I'd look out for that rather nice skirt, if I were you. It won't last half an hour in this place."

"I see." Protective instincts on full alert, Nicole drew Tommy to her and stroked his hair. "Where is the Commander?"

"Having a word with Miss Janet. We won't be here for dinner, which I daresay will displease her no end."

"I see," Nicole said again, not at all sure she liked what she was, in fact, seeing. From her expression and tone, it was clear the woman cared for Janet about as much as she cared for children, which wasn't much.

The silence which ensued might have grown a little awkward had it not been broken by the sound of footsteps marching down the hall. A moment later, the Commander reappeared.

"Oh, here you are, sweets." The woman rose up in a swirl of rose-patterned silk and went to meet him, chucking Tommy under the chin as she passed by. She was tall, perhaps five feet nine or ten, most of which seemed apportioned to her legs, which were enviable. "Your Nanny's come back and our little boy's quite safe, aren't you, Thomas?"

The Commander smiled tightly. "It never occurred to me he wasn't, Louise. I take it you've introduced yourself to Miss Bennett?"

"Not formally." Louise slipped her arm through his and fluttered her long lashes. "But we've chatted and I think she'll be wonderful for the job, Pierce. You can see already how taken she is with Thomas and he with her."

"I agree." Detaching himself from the thin fingers clutching at him, he gestured to Tommy. "Will you take him to the playroom for a few minutes, while I conclude matters with Miss Bennett?"

The ghost of a grimace soured Louise's smile. "If you promise not to take too long. I'm presenting an offer on the Willingdon property at four and have another show-ing at five.''

"Ten minutes," he said, and waited until she'd taken Tommy away before turning to Nicole. "Well, Miss Bennett, are you still interested in becoming a nanny?"

"Absolutely, Commander Warner. Tommy is delight-ful.''

He nodded and strode behind the desk. "Good. Then the job's yours if the terms I've laid out here are agree-able to you."

He handed her a contract which, for appearances' sake, she pretended to scrutinize. In fact, she'd have worked for nothing if that's what he'd asked, but the salary he was proposing to pay her was generous in the extreme.

"This is more than satisfactory, Commander," she said, deciding that most of what she earned would go into a trust fund for Tommy.

"Then we have a deal." He scrawled his name at the bottom of the page, then offered the pen to her. When she'd signed, he reached out to shake her hand again, another brief, businesslike clasp such as he'd offered when she'd first met him. "I'll expect you tomorrow morning. Will ten o'clock suit you?"

"Actually," she said, trying not to sound overeager, "I can start tonight, if you like. Your friend mentioned that you were dining out and I'd be happy to baby-sit."

He looked pleasantly surprised. "Thank you. I'm sure Janet will appreciate having the evening off."

"Then I'll go and collect my things." Nicole flicked a glance at the clock on the mantelpiece. "I have a few odds and ends to take care of, but I can be back here by six."

"Thank you again. I'll warn Janet to expect you for dinner and leave her to show you to your suite of rooms."

"Fine." She picked up her bag from where she'd left

it on the floor next to the desk. "I'll see you later, Commander."

She walked demurely along the hall and out through the front door. Climbed into her car, drove sedately down the driveway, and waited until the house was hidden behind a belt of trees before giving vent to the pent-up sigh of relief that was stretching her lungs to bursting.

She was home free! Provided she could keep her grief under wraps, the rest would be easy. Once she'd allayed any fears her employer might have regarding her motives, she could erase the lies and half-truths by which she'd gained access to Tommy and present herself for who she really was: his dead mother's long-lost sister.

In the meantime, she had shopping to do. She'd come with party clothes, the sort of things a woman packed when she thought she was embarking on a holiday reunion. Sandals, sundresses, cocktail gowns. Beaded bags and diamond studs, spindle heels and sheer silk lingerie. And Pierce Warner's lady friend was right: such a wardrobe no more fit the role of nanny than that of coffee shop waitress.

She needed clothes to fit the part. Denim skirts and trim white blouses. Cotton shorts and tops. Flat-heeled sandals and a plain bathrobe to replace the French silk peignoir lurking in the bottom of her suitcase.

The only things she didn't need to acquire were a bottomless well of sympathy, an endless supply of tears, of love, of gut-wrenching pity. Those she already had in abundance. She could only hope they'd be enough.

"Pierce, that's the fourth time you've looked at your watch in the last fifteen minutes and I'm beginning to feel neglected."

"Sorry." He drummed up a smile and touched his glass to Louise's in a toast. "I didn't realize I was being so obvious."

"Sweetness, the woman is clearly as trustworthy as Mother Teresa. She was practically drooling all over

Thomas when they came back from the beach and he seemed just as enthralled with her. It's obviously a match made in heaven.''

"I agree. It's the reason behind her being hired that I'm having a tough time coming to grips with. It just hasn't sunk in yet that Jim and Arlene won't be coming back.''

"I know. I can't believe it, either.''

He shook his head, impatient with himself. "Death doesn't get any easier to accept. I'm still haunted by that kid I lost on my last deployment. Now losing Jim, too—'' He bowed his head, his chest aching. "I feel so bloody helpless.''

Louise shifted closer on the banquette until her knee was rubbing against his and her breast nudged his arm. "Pierce, stop it! That seaman's death was no more your fault than your cousin's accident was. Sadly, these things happen sometimes but the best thing we can do is go on with our lives. And, sweetie, you've become very much a part of mine. You do know that, don't you?''

She increased the pressure on his arm, reminding him that she had very nice breasts indeed, and looked at him from eyes grown heavy-lidded with promise. He felt his own flesh tightening in response and suddenly wished they were alone instead of in a restaurant, and that he could lose himself inside her. Perhaps then he would forget, if only for a few minutes, the picture of Jim and Arlene as they'd looked when he'd gone to identify the bodies.

"How hungry are you, Louise?''

They'd become lovers about a month ago and she knew exactly what prompted the question. "Starving,'' she purred, rolling her martini olive into her mouth with the tip of her tongue. "But not for chateaubriand. Let's go, Pierce.''

She lived about half a mile from him, in a house she'd spent a small fortune renovating. Everything about it, from its marble-floored entry to the gold faucets in her bathroom to the dozen or so water candles arranged around her bed, reflected her sybaritic tastes. "There are glasses and champagne chilling," she cooed, nodding at the bar refrigerator concealed in the lacquered wall unit at one end of her bedroom. "I'll be back in a moment."

He opened the champagne, stood it in a bucket of ice, then lit six of the candles. Strolling to the window, he loosened his tie and checked his watch one more time. Almost twenty-one hundred hours. Was Tom settled for the night? Should he phone to make sure everything was going smoothly with the new nanny?

She was a pretty little thing and seemed capable enough. Not that the two were related, but it seemed to him that it would be easier for a kid of four to take to someone who looked a bit like his mother than it would to someone old enough to be his grandmother.

Not that the dark-haired, dark-eyed Miss Bennett bore much resemblance to Arlene, who'd been blond. But they were about the same age and of similar height and build. Though perhaps the nanny weighed a couple of pounds less—about a hundred and ten, he figured, and they hung remarkably well on her five foot, five inch frame.

"Why, Pierce, here I am all ready to be seduced and you haven't even gotten around to removing your shoes!"

Louise swanned back into the room, half dressed in one of those floating negligee things that revealed more than it covered and which he'd previously seen only on posters pinned up in lockers aboard ship. All he had to do was tug lightly on the piece of ribbon holding it closed and the whole contraption would slide down around her feet. The thought, coupled with the amount of exquisite ivory flesh already on display, should have left him straining for release.

It didn't.

"I'll pour the champagne," he said, and knew, from the way she flounced over to the bed and spread herself out against the pillows, that she was disappointed by his delaying tactics.

"Aren't you going to join me, darling?" she pouted, accepting her glass of champagne. "It's lonely in this big old bed without you."

Before he could stop himself, he glanced again at his watch.

"It's only five past nine, Pierce," she protested, sighing audibly. "No one's going to report you AWOL if you stay out another hour or two."

She was ticked off and he couldn't blame her. "Sorry," he said yet again, dropping down beside her on the bed and stuffing a pillow behind his head. She was the only woman he'd ever met who actually used satin sheets. He found them very slippery.

"You're forgiven." She smiled, a lazy, sexy smile, and leaned over to unbutton his shirt. "Just don't let it happen again."

Her hands were cool and very skillful. Were the nanny's? Would she handle Tom gently when she lifted him out of his bath?

He shook his head irritably. Of course she would! She was a nurse, for Pete's sake!

"Come back, sweetness," Louise whispered, raking her long fingernails over his chest with just enough pressure to indicate she didn't care for his preoccupation.

"Hey," he said, trapping her hand, as a thought occurred to him, "is the phone turned on in here? I mean, if anyone wanted to get hold of me, would they be able to get through?"

"Pierce," she said, on another long-suffering sigh, "I'm in real estate. Have you ever known my phone *not* to be turned on?"

"No," he admitted wryly. They'd been in the middle of making love for the first time when she'd received a call from a client wishing to view a house she'd just listed. Apart from being a touch out of breath throughout the conversation, she'd managed to set up the appointment without missing a beat. He hadn't known whether to be flattered or insulted.

"Then why," she said now, "don't you just relax and make us both enjoy ourselves?"

She had the most delicious legs this side of a chorus line. A man would have to be dead not to respond to the lure of them. "Right," he said, taking her glass and placing it beside his own on the night table. "We've wasted enough time on small talk."

"Thank God you finally got the message," she breathed, leaning forward to touch his nipple with her tongue. "Take your pants off, Pierce, darling. Although I love a man in uniform, a charcoal lounge suit doesn't do a whole lot for me at a time like this."

Her hands slid to the buckle of his belt, adding urgency to her request. It should have been enough to trigger the response she was seeking. Tonight, it wasn't—a fact she'd discover for herself soon enough.

Cupping her face, he kissed her with great determination. Her lips were lush as ripe strawberries. Her skin smelled of Paris, very chic, very French—as it should, considering the imported hand-milled soap she used and the perfume specially brought in for her by Marshall Fields in Chicago. Her hair, a rich red-gold, glowed like a flame. Unfortunately, none of the aforementioned set him on fire.

Finally, he pulled away, took her hands in his and held her at a distance. "We're trying too hard, Louise."

"Why, Pierce," she murmured, pouting again. "Have I lost my touch?"

"It's not your fault," he said, his glance sliding yet again to his watch. "I've got too many things on my mind right now."

"And I'm obviously not one of them." She drained her glass, clearly annoyed.

He could hardly blame her. They were in her bed at his suggestion, after all. "Let me just call home," he began. "Once I know—"

"Oh, forget it!" She flounced off the bed and splashed more wine into her glass. "Frankly, you're not the only one no longer in the mood. Good night, Pierce. Call me when you get your act together."

There was a light showing at the nanny's bedroom window when he got home. Treading softly so as not to disturb Tom, who'd been sleeping very restlessly all week, Pierce stopped outside her door, surprised to see it standing ajar. He'd assumed she was in bed already but she sat instead in the little sitting room that faced the back of the house and looked out to sea.

She wore a long blue dressing gown and had white furry slippers on her feet. Her dark brown hair hung around her shoulders in soft waves, and her face was scrubbed clean of what little makeup she'd worn earlier. She was reading a letter and several others lay in her lap. She held a steaming cup in one hand.

Suddenly, she glanced up and did a double take when she found herself being watched. He saw then that she'd been crying.

"Sorry," he muttered, pushing the door open a little farther. "I didn't mean to intrude. I just got home and wondered how you'd managed with Tom. You seem upset. Did he give you a hard time?"

"No," she said, making an effort to compose herself. "It's not that at all. He was as good as gold."

He shrugged helplessly. He never quite knew what to do with weeping women; they weren't too common on board a naval destroyer. "Well, if it's not Tom, then what? Are you having second thoughts about the job?"

"No." Setting her cup on the table in front of her, she fished a wad of tissues from her pocket and dabbed at her eyes. She was silent for so long that he thought the conversation had come to an end when she seemed to reach a decision of some sort and spoke again. "I think, Commander Warner, that there's something you ought to know."

"I'm listening," he said, bracing himself. She had a look about her that spelled trouble.

She plucked a fresh tissue from the box at her elbow and blew her nose. "I haven't been exactly truthful, I'm afraid."

It wasn't exactly the sort of news he appreciated hearing! Pretty direct himself, he hadn't much use for people who weren't equally up-front in their dealings. "In what respect, Miss Bennett?"

"Well..." She stopped and chanced a quick glance at him.

He held her gaze relentlessly. "Please continue."

Her chin wobbled dangerously. "Recently, I... suffered...um...um...."

What? he was tempted to bark at her. *A spell in prison for child abuse? A nervous breakdown? A malpractice suit for dereliction of duty?*

"Something happened," she said, and dropped her gaze to the letters in her lap.

Of course! She'd received a Dear John—or was it a Dear Jane for a woman? Either way, he thought he'd figured out what had brought on the tears. He'd seen it happen before enough times to recognize the symptoms. Otherwise fearless men brought to their knees by a one-page letter telling them they were history in some woman's life.

"So that's why you left Minnesota," he said.

She looked up him, her dark brown eyes wide and startled. "What?"

"You wanted to make a fresh start."

"Yes," she said, eyeing him suspiciously. "But I'd already decided to do that before..."

The waterworks were about to start again. "Before he broke your heart," he finished for her, deciding a quick, clean cut was kinder than letting her linger in misery.

She continued to stare at him as if she thought he was slightly mad. "No. Someone in my family died."

"Oh," he said, and then, insensitive clod that he was, added, "I assumed some guy had dumped you."

She gave a watery laugh at that. "No, nothing quite that simple, I'm afraid."

"I'm sorry, Miss Bennett, I didn't mean to make light of your loss."

A fresh load of tears sparkled in her eyes. "My emotions are very close to the surface right now."

"I fully appreciate that." Uninvited, he advanced into the room and perched on the windowsill. "What can I do to make things easier for you?"

She shook her head, which was enough to send the tears flying down her cheeks. "Nothing."

Should he lend a shoulder for her to cry on? Pat her back? Stroke her pretty hair and murmur words of comfort?

The thought stirred him more thoroughly than his earlier bedroom encounter with Louise. Hurriedly, he handed over a fresh tissue and wished he'd waited until the morning to have this conversation. "What's that you're drinking?"

"Herbal tea," she said. "I thought it might help me sleep. I hope you don't mind that I made myself at home in the kitchen."

"Not in the least, but how about a shot of brandy instead?"

"No, thank you. I don't drink much."

"That's good," he said. A closet tippler was the last thing he—or Tom—needed! "It might not be a bad idea to make an exception just this once, though. In fact, I could use a drink myself."

Before she could raise further objections, he stuffed another tissue in her hand and made his escape. On his way downstairs, he poked his head into Tom's room. He was fast asleep. From behind her door, Janet's rhythmic snoring told him all was well on that front, also.

By the time he returned to the nanny's room, she'd got the tears under control. Even though her eyes had a bruised look about them, she managed to drum up a smile.

"Here," he said, offering her the snifter. "Down the hatch with this and you'll sleep like a baby, I promise."

She took a sip and grimaced. "I do apologize, Commander Warner. I'm not usually such an emotional mess."

"Why didn't you say something this afternoon? Did you think I'd reject your application, because you've suffered a family bereavement?"

She hesitated before replying and he thought an expression of near-guilt crossed her face, but it was such a fleeting thing that he couldn't be sure. "Private details don't belong in interviews," she said finally.

"They do sometimes, especially if they affect a person's ability to cope with her duties."

"Oh, I won't allow that to happen!" she exclaimed, a flush of alarm tinting her pale face. "I'd *never* do anything to jeopardize Tommy's well-being."

She looked so earnest, and so damned soft and appealing that he was startled to find himself again inclined to draw her into his arms and comfort her. To preclude any such action, he downed the rest of his brandy, stood up to leave, and said, "I believe you, Miss Bennett."

"Do you? Really?"

"Every word."

Why didn't she look reassured at that? What caused her to gnaw uneasily on her lip, as though he'd handed her a gift she didn't deserve?

"Look," he said, "I understand only too well the void left behind when someone dies but the only way to get past it is to go forward, because standing still and looking back at what we've lost is just too painful."

She got up from the chair and pressed her hands together. He noticed they were every bit as fine and soft as he'd expected them to be. "You're right. Thank you, Commander. I swear you won't regret entrusting Tommy to my care."

"I don't expect to. Good night, Miss Bennett."

He'd turned away and was almost at the door when she stopped him with one last request. "Won't you please call me Nicole?"

Strange, the effect the request had on him. There was something forlorn in her voice that told him more clearly than anything she'd actually put into words that she was hurting badly and fighting with every ounce of grit she could muster to cope with the pain.

"Nicole," he echoed, hearing the cadence of her name on his tongue and liking how it sounded.

Embarrassed to find himself staring into her eyes as if he'd been hypnotized, he cleared his throat and said brusquely, "Well, if we're dropping the formalities and I suppose, since you're more or less part of the family now, we might as well, I'm Pierce."

"Yes." She smiled a little. "The name suits you."

Instinct told him not to ask, but curiosity got the better of him. "How so?"

"Everything about you is very direct. A woman knows where she stands with you and I admire that in a man."

There were a few things he admired about her, too. Her hair, for instance, and the classic oval of her face. And her long, dark lashes. If it weren't for the fact that she'd washed or wept away her makeup, he might have thought they were false or coated with eye shadow, or whatever it was women put on them for effect. In any event, they added drama to her already lovely eyes.

But it was more than just her face that he found appealing, he admitted, allowing his gaze to roam over the rest of her. She had the sort of slight build that brought a man's protective urges to the fore. Her waist was narrow as a child's, her hips a mere suggestion beneath the blue dressing gown, and her breasts...were none of his concern.

He cleared his throat again. "Yes, well, good night, Nicole."

"Good night, Pierce."

"Sleep well."

"I'll try."

Shutting the door after him, Nicole leaned against it and let out a slow breath of relief. How could she have come so close to blowing her cover, knowing as she did what she had to lose by doing so? The thing was, he'd caught her in a moment of weakness and that, combined with his sympathy, had almost undone her.

She'd realized her mistake at once. There'd been no misinterpreting his wariness at the idea of her having lied. Quite how he'd have reacted if she'd finished what she'd started to say didn't bear thinking about. She'd probably be packing her bags by now.

It was just as well that, after all, she'd chosen to ignore her mother's warning when they'd spoken on the phone earlier.

"You're not thinking straight," Nancy Bennett had sighed, when Nicole unfolded her plan. "You went to Oregon expecting to reunite with a sister you'd lost touch with years ago, only to find you'd lost her all over again—permanently, this time—and the whole tragedy is taking its toll on you. Come clean now, honey, before the lies trip you up."

At first, she'd been inclined to heed the advice but Tommy had changed her mind. Confronted by Pierce's sympathy and with the truth practically trembling on her lips, she'd had a sudden memory flash of the evening she and the child had spent together and made a split-second choice: being with him was worth any amount of deception.

They'd bonded instantly, the way an aunt and nephew should. Everything about him enchanted her—his speech, his four-year-old mannerisms, his curiosity and trust. She loved how he prefaced almost every remark to her with her name.

"Nicole?" he'd said, as they sat at dinner.

"Yes, darling?"

"Are you going to live here tonight?"

"Yes, darling," she'd said, mopping up the small puddle of milk he'd spilled. "And tomorrow night, as well."

"Oh." He'd regarded her from big eyes, and digested that bit of information with the last of his macaroni cheese. "Nicole?"

"Yes, sweetheart?"

"Will you sleep with Uncle Pierce?"

She'd almost choked on her own food at that. "No, Tommy."

"Why not?"

"Because I have my own bed in my own room."

"Mommy sleeps with Daddy."

Oh, precious, I hope so! I hope wherever they are that they're together and that they know I'll keep you safe for them. She'd swallowed the familiar rush of tears and said simply, "I know. They keep each other company."

"Nicole?"

"Yes, Tommy?"

"In the morning, we can go swimming."

"That would be nice."

"But only if you're there. Uncle Pierce says it's very, very dangerous to go in the pool by myself."

"He's right. Now, if you're finished eating, how about we clear the table to save Janet having to do it?"

"All right." He'd hopped down from his chair and carried his plate and glass to the counter next to the sink. After she'd rinsed them, he showed her how he could load them into the dishwasher. It had been all she could do not to smother him with hugs and kisses.

Janet, who'd been ironing at the other end of the kitchen, had observed the interaction but made no comment. "I'm here if you need me," she'd said, when Nicole asked why she hadn't joined them for dinner, "but it's best if the two of you spend time alone together and get to know one another as quickly as possible. Poor motherless mite, he needs someone who can give him all her attention for a while, and I can't, it's as simple as that. I'm just glad you came along when you did.''

Nicole had warmed to the housekeeper for the trust implicit in her words. She'd bathed Tommy and read him a story, then sat with him until he'd fallen asleep. Those last few minutes had been precious in their intimacy.

"Nicole?" he'd said, clutching his dee-dee.

She stroked a finger up his cheek, "Yes, darling?"

"Is Mommy coming home tomorrow?"

What she wouldn't have given to be able to say yes. And what she wouldn't do to make sure he'd never have to wonder if *she*'d be there for him in the morning. "No, sweetheart, but I'll be here."

His eyes had clouded and she'd folded him in her arms, her heart aching with a pain that could be assuaged only by holding that little boy as close to her as possible, and hoping that, in easing his sorrow, perhaps she'd find a little relief for herself. "What would you like for breakfast when you wake up, Tommy?"

"Pancakes," he'd murmured drowsily. "And brown syrup."

"Then pancakes it'll be."

And it was. Every day for the rest of that week.

Pierce always had breakfast with them and was often there for dinner, too. "Is all that stuff good for him?" he asked, on the third morning. "Shouldn't he be eating something more wholesome, like porridge, and forget about the syrup?"

"Not when the weather's so hot, Pierce. Porridge is winter food. As for the syrup, I give him only a minimal amount. As long as he brushes his teeth, it won't do him any harm."

"Well, you're the nurse," he'd said doubtfully. "I suppose you know what you're doing."

But he didn't really believe that and continued to keep

tabs on her and question her about everything, from the number of times a day that she changed Tommy's clothes to the amount of time it took him to polish off a meal.

"Twenty minutes should be enough for anyone to clean his plate," he claimed irritably, on the Friday evening when Tommy was particularly slow to finish his main course. "My crew could get through four times that amount of food in half the time he takes."

"Since he's not in the Navy," she replied tartly, "I hardly think it matters. In any case, mealtimes shouldn't be reduced to races to see who can cross the finishing line first. They should be social occasions."

Pierce had let the subject lie but the look he gave her across the table reminded her that she could push him only so far. In the final analysis, he *was* the boss and she made a mental note not to forget it. She wouldn't have been able to bear it if he'd fired her.

The next eight weeks sped by, and if the ache of losing her sister didn't exactly disappear, it was made easier for Nicole to bear by getting to know her nephew. Tommy was such an easy child to love. So willing to please, so sweet-tempered, so affectionate. And apart from that one near-disastrous confession her first night on the job, she fit into her role of nanny without a hitch. No one, she was sure, had any inkling that the affection she lavished on Tommy stemmed from anything other than pure dedication to the job she'd been hired to do.

So why, as one fear lessened, did another kind of uneasiness take its place? Why wasn't the fact that she had unlimited access to her nephew, that she had a more or less free hand in how she went about her responsibilities, and that she lived in a gorgeous house in a breathtaking setting, enough to make her as happy as could be expected?

The answer wasn't one she cared to dwell on, but there really wasn't any escaping it. Pierce Warner was the problem. Not because he frequently seemed to forget that he wasn't in the Navy any longer and didn't realize that four-year-old boys weren't miniature underlings with a built-in respect for strict adherence to rules and regulations. *That* Nicole could and did handle, but diplomatically—not just because she didn't want to put her job at risk, but also because the last thing Tommy needed at that point in his life was two adults squabbling in front of him.

What she couldn't swallow with any sort of equanimity were the twinges of envy that attacked without warning every time Louise Trent showed up and lay claim to Pierce with a determination that couldn't have been made clearer if she'd stood on the roof and screamed to the whole world: "Hands off! This man is mine!"

Equally difficult to stomach was the fact that, while she plowed around the house suitably dressed-down as befit a nanny, Louise flaunted her assets shamelessly. She wore silk which never wrinkled, no matter how hot the day; delicate strappy sandals with heels as fine as wineglass stems. To showcase her sinfully beautiful legs, her hemlines never rode a fraction of an inch lower than mid-thigh, regardless of the weather.

And speaking of which, while Louise protected her porcelain complexion beneath wide-brimmed hats made of the finest panama, Nicole grew as brown as newly baked bread from chasing Tommy around the garden and along the beach. Truly, she felt every inch the peasant servant in contrast to Louise who clearly saw herself as lady of the manor.

Nicole tried to rationalize her feelings the best way she knew how. She told herself that they arose because Tommy deserved to have Pierce to himself more often, instead of having to make do with a quick visit sandwiched between the end of his uncle's working day and Louise's plans for the evening.

But that line of reasoning fell apart when she found herself lying awake waiting to hear the sound of the automatic garage door opener heralding Pierce's late night return from his date, and wondering how serious he was about Louise, if they were sleeping together.

Once the questions entered her head, there was no escaping them and, to her shame, she found a way to get the answers. One morning in early July when Janet joined her on the patio for midmorning coffee, she said, with what she prayed would come across as nothing more than idle curiosity, "Are the Commander and Miss Trent planning to get married soon?"

"If she gets her way, they will," Janet replied sourly. "That woman sank her chicken-pluckers into him, the minute she set eyes on him."

"Oh," Nicole said, her spirits plummeting absurdly. "They've known each other some time, then?"

"About six months. They met when he came home for good and started shopping for a place to live. She found this house for him and made herself generally indispensable in the process."

Nicole smiled. It wasn't the first time Janet had intimated her dislike of Pierce's lady friend. "Where will you fit in, if she becomes Mrs. Warner?"

"I won't," Janet replied, without hesitation. "I'll hand in notice before she gets the chance to fire me. I was housekeeper for the Commander's parents from the time he turned fourteen, and I'd gladly work for him 'til I drop in my tracks, but that hussy...!"

She snorted disparagingly, then gave way to a gleeful smile. "Of course, things aren't going as smoothly as she'd like anymore," she remarked, nodding to where Tommy played in his sandbox. "Inheriting someone else's child isn't part of her plan, for all that she puts on such a fine act when the Commander's around to see it. But I guess you've gathered that much for yourself, Nicole. You don't strike me as someone who misses much when it comes to that boy."

"No. In fact, that's what prompted me to ask if the relationship's serious," Nicole said, and tried to believe the allegation was true. What sort of idiot allowed herself to moon after a man already in love with someone else, after all?

But the envy continued regardless. Became more like plain, green-eyed jealousy, in fact. And without knowing how it happened, she found being with Tommy wasn't quite enough to fill all her needs. Sometimes, she ached for a man's arms around her, for a man's lips to be pressed to hers.

Specifically, she wanted Pierce's strong, tanned arms around her, and his broad shoulder to lean on. She wanted his gaze to settle on her lips with the same hungry curiosity that hers glommed onto his. He had a very handsome mouth; strong, finely sculpted, sexy.

She was so ashamed of herself, so mortified. Her only consolation lay in the fact that he had no idea how she felt about him.

Unfortunately, Louise Trent did.

CHAPTER THREE

NICOLE had long believed women were more intuitive than men, and Louise proved herself no exception. Her built-in radar started picking up danger signals almost as soon as Nicole herself realized the direction in which things were headed, and her cordiality shrank proportionately.

At first, she tried to direct her attack through Pierce. "Grief, sweets," she trilled, the Saturday she arrived unexpectedly and found him sharing peanut butter and jelly sandwiches by the pool with Nicole and Tommy, "what a good thing I decided to stop by and let you take me out to lunch."

"Why don't you join us instead?" Pierce suggested, pulling up a chair for her. "We've got plenty of food and iced tea."

Louise inspected the sandwiches as if she expected to find roach tracks in the peanut butter, and shuddered. "They're serving fresh Dungeness crab salad and chardonnay at the yacht club, Pierce."

"Sorry, Louise," he said. "I promised Tommy I'd give him a swimming lesson this afternoon."

She swept a glance over the scene, her eyes beneath the brim of her black straw hat coldly assessing. Nicole could imagine what sort of tableau the three of them made, lounging at leisure amid an assortment of towels, sunscreen lotion and inflatable water toys. To the uninitiated, they might have been the perfect, close-knit family, with Louise the interloper. And that clearly was not a picture the visitor relished.

"Why you, Pierce?" she inquired.

42

He shrugged his decidedly splendid shoulders. "Why not me?"

"Because," she said peevishly, "I fail to see the point in hiring a dog if you have to bark yourself."

It was a calculated insult made all the more offensive by her studied appraisal of Nicole, which Pierce didn't miss. The family man image refocused to reveal his other persona, the naval officer unused to having his decisions questioned.

He put down the sandwich he was about to bite into, fixed her in a stare that only a fool would have perceived as anything other than highly dangerous, then brought his gaze to bear on Nicole. "*Dog*, Louise?"

The August afternoon crackled with unspoken hostility. Feeling suddenly and indecently exposed beneath the scrutiny, Nicole found herself reaching surreptitiously for her cotton cover-up, even though her one-piece swimsuit was modestly cut.

Tommy shattered the tension. "Where's a dog?" he asked hopefully, looking around.

"It's just a figure of speech, Thomas," Louise said. "There isn't really a dog here."

But although she laughed merrily, the glint in her eyes was every bit as steely as that in Pierce's, leaving Nicole in no doubt that the woman who'd started out as her ally no longer regarded her with favor.

The hint of a smile relaxed the stern line of Pierce's mouth. "Well, perhaps there should be," he said. "How would you feel, Nicole, about our taking on a puppy?"

"I think that would be wonderful," she said, unable to quell her pleasure at the way he phrased the question, as if he, too, was beginning to think of her as part of the family. "I'm game for anything that helps Tommy get through the next few months."

Louise looked as if she might explode, though whether that was because she objected to dogs in general or only those she perceived as invading her territory was a moot point. "Oh, Pierce!" she exclaimed. "Do you really think that's wise? I mean, sweetie, think about it. Dog hair all over everything, and muddy paw prints.'' She wrinkled her nose fastidiously. ''Not to mention accidents on the carpets.''

Tommy's ears perked up again, less enthusiastically this time. ''Mommy and Daddy had an accident,'' he said worriedly, leaning against Nicole's knee. ''They aren't coming home ever again.''

''Oh, Tommy,'' Nicole said, drawing him onto her lap, ''that was a different kind of accident. If we got a puppy, nothing bad would happen to it. Uncle Pierce and I would make sure of that.''

''I'm talking about the sort of accident where an animal goes to the toilet in inappropriate places, Thomas,'' Louise cut in, sending Nicole the sort of killing glare meant to stunt any other promises she might feel disposed to make.

But Tommy clung to Nicole, winding his arms so anxiously around her neck that she felt constrained to point out, ''You're confusing him, Miss Trent. He's only just turned four and is having a tough enough time coping with the upheaval in his life. We need to be careful that we don't inadvertently increase his apprehensions.''

''Thank you for your input, Miss Bennett,'' came the sarcastic reply. ''I can't imagine how we've managed without it this long. Pierce, are you sure you won't let me coax you into lunch at the club?''

''Not today, Louise,'' he said, hoisting Tommy off Nicole's lap and onto his shoulder. ''A promise is a promise, and it's time for that swimming lesson. But you go ahead.''

''I will,'' she said, smiling fixedly. ''I'll just visit with Miss Bennett for a few minutes first, and watch the swimming lesson.'' She blew him a kiss. ''See you later, around six?''

''Sure.''

The second he was out of earshot, she launched her offensive. ''So tell me,'' she purred, ''do you always take such a personal interest in your patients, Miss Bennett?''

"Yes," Nicole said. "Although I don't exactly see Tommy as a patient."

"No? Then how do you see him?" Louise crossed her elegant legs and swung a negligent ankle.

"I'm not sure I follow you."

"Oh, I think you do, my dear." She rooted in her bag, withdrew a mirrored compact and proceeded to touch up her already flawless mouth with a carmine lip pencil. "Your attachment to Thomas is unnatural. No one walks into a house and takes to a child as you apparently have to him—instantaneously, as it were—unless she has a hidden agenda." Sunlight dazzled briefly in the reflection from the compact mirror as she snapped it closed. "Just between us women, Nicole, what is it you really want from this job?"

Despite the sun, Nicole went cold, afraid she'd somehow tipped her hand and that the other woman had guessed her secret. But then common sense prevailed. Louise wasn't interested in Tommy; Pierce was her only concern. "There's no hidden agenda, Miss Trent. I'm merely bringing to this position the same dedication I've brought to others I've held."

"So the child is the drawing card?"

"Yes."

"And Pierce?"

Certainly no one could ever accuse Louise Trent of skirting an issue! She delivered the question in the form of a challenge, her attractive hazel eyes laser sharp as they tracked Nicole's face where the beginnings of a blush threatened.

Quickly, before it gave her away completely, Nicole sprang to her feet and began stacking the lunch dishes. "The Commander is merely my employer."

It was true. He'd done nothing, said nothing, to lead her to believe otherwise. His primary consideration was making a home for Tommy and she was merely an accessory to that end. An entirely disposable accessory, should she not perform satisfactorily.

In the clear light of day, her nighttime thoughts about him showed up for what they were: ridiculous fantasies of the kind that junior nurses often harbored about doctors and which she liked to think she'd outgrown years ago. Louise Trent need fear nothing from her. "I love children," she said. "I have devoted my entire adult life to them."

"Very noble of you, I'm sure," Louise replied silkily. "And very clever, too."

"Clever?"

"Well, my dear, Pierce would have a difficult time justifying your presence here if Thomas shrieked every time he set eyes on you, now wouldn't he? As it is, he's indebted to you." There followed a small, calculated pause. "As am I. Your competence and dedication allow Pierce and me to pursue our private relationship without fear that Thomas is being neglected. We are both very grateful. I'm sure you understand what I'm saying?"

"Perfectly." Nicole held the stare directed her way without flinching. "Three's a crowd."

Louise Trent's smile was about as subtle as a tiger drawing back its lips to reveal its teeth. "Very good, dear! I so dislike having to belabor a point. You're a perceptive woman, Nicole."

I'm a liar, Nicole thought, watching Louise walk away. I'm lying to everyone, including myself. And I can't afford to make an enemy of a woman who, if she ever uncovered my deceit, would cut me up in little pieces and serve me to Pierce on a platter.

"Hey, Nicole!" Pierce waved from the shallow end of the pool, his dark hair slicked down and gleaming with water. Tommy bobbed at his side, squealing with glee. "Somebody here wants your company."

Temptation beckoned. Where was the harm, after all? And wasn't this what she'd been hired to do: stand in as the mother figure for a little boy who'd lost both parents?

Yes, the voice of common sense agreed. But not if, in the process, you forget that Pierce Warner's role stops short of being your mate. He's seeing another woman. He'll be spending the evening with her—maybe the whole night. Three isn't really a crowd here. It's just that, job description notwithstanding, you're not the third member of the party. Louise Trent is, and she won't willingly abdicate the spot.

"Come on, Nicole. What's keeping you?"

Although the effort made her teeth ache, she smiled and picked up the lunch dishes. "I promised to help Janet pick raspberries for dessert tonight. I'll take over later while you get ready to go out."

He shrugged the broad, tanned shoulders which recently had occupied far too much of her attention. "If that's what you want."

It wasn't. But what she wanted wasn't hers to have.

He didn't come home until after one the next morning. Not that Nicole spent the entire time clock watching, but Tommy had woken up crying and she just happened to be on her way to his room when Pierce appeared at the top of the stairs.

"What is it?" he asked in a low voice, striding down the hall toward her. "Is Tom sick or something?"

"I think he's having one of his bad dreams. The monitor picked up the sound of him crying out."

"Poor kid," Pierce murmured sympathetically. "Want me to lend a hand getting him settled?"

"I can manage on my own."

"I'm sure you can, Nicole, but he might feel better having both of us there to reassure him."

Hunching her shoulders, she said, "Suit yourself," and couldn't resist adding, "if you're not too tired, that is."

He could hardly have missed the sarcasm in her voice

but she didn't give him time to take issue with it. Slipping past him, she hurried into Tommy's room.

He lay in a tangle of covers, with his face flushed and damp with tears. "It's too dark," he sobbed. "I want my mommy."

Nicole swept him into her arms and rocked him. "Tommy, darling, wake up. You were dreaming again, but I'm here now."

"Mommy forgot me," he wailed. "She left me by myself."

"You're not by yourself, darling. Uncle Pierce is here and so am I." The tears were dribbling down her face, too; tears of grief and tears of helplessness. How could anyone hope to fill the awful gaping hole left in a child's life when neither of his parents would ever come home to him again?

"Let me try," Pierce said, perching on the other side of the bed and reaching for Tommy.

But Tommy would have none of him. Heartbroken, he clutched his dee-dee and hid his face against Nicole's neck. Obviously at a loss, Pierce paced restlessly across the room, then came back to the bed. "What can I do?" he muttered, almost to himself. "If I knew what it was, I'd do it, no matter what it cost."

"Be here for him, Pierce," Nicole said, understanding his frustration and sharing it. "Love him. It's all any of us can do."

A spasm of anger crossed his face. "It isn't enough. He needs his mother and father. He *deserves* them."

"Yes." She pressed her hand to the back of Tommy's head and continued to rock him against her shoulder. The sobs were subsiding, but the occasional shudder still racked his little body.

Pierce watched, his expression grim. "So help me, if anyone ever hurts this kid again..." He swallowed and shook his head. "...they'd better stay clear of me, because I don't think I'd find myself disposed to be merciful."

Of course it wasn't a warning directed at her. Rationally, Nicole knew that. Yet the specter of her deception loomed between them, darker and more momentous than ever. How would he react if—*when* he found out?

"Why don't you go to bed?" she said, afraid suddenly of what that observant gaze of his might uncover. "There's no sense in both of us staying up."

"I'll wait until he's calmer."

"After one of these nightmares, it often takes about an hour before he drops off again."

"You intend to stay with him until he's asleep?"

"Of course."

"And what if he doesn't settle? What if you're up half the night with him?"

"I'll take him into my bed with me, if I have to."

"Are you sure that's a good idea?"

"Why not?" she whispered defensively. "He's only four years old. What possible harm can it do?"

He reared back in mild reproof. "No need to get your hackles up, Nicole."

"It strikes me as a small enough concession if it helps him get past his parents' death, and aren't you the one who just said you'd go to any lengths to try to make things up to him?"

"I just wonder if we aren't setting ourselves up for trouble if we let that sort of thing become a habit, that's all."

They were close enough that echoes of his aftershave drifted over her. As if that weren't distraction enough, she noticed that at some point in the evening, he'd removed his tie. It was stuffed in the pocket of his tan blazer now, the end of it dangling in plain view and taunting her to the point of foolhardiness. How else to account for the reckless remark that fell out of her mouth before she could prevent it? "That sounds like the sort of argument your friend Louise would come up with."

"As a matter of fact, we have discussed it."

"*It?*" she spat. "What *it?*"

"Your devotion to Tom. Your patience. How quickly you've come to love him. Louise mentioned only tonight what a remarkable woman you are but she did wonder if perhaps you aren't spoiling him a bit." He watched her closely, his eyes inky blue in the subdued glow cast by the small night-light on the wall next to Tommy's bed. "Does that bother you?"

Everything about Louise Trent bothers me, she was tempted to shriek, *most especially the fact that you've come home half undressed after spending the last six hours in her company.* "Not at all," she said, with commendable restraint. "The last I heard, we still live in a democracy and a person is entitled to her opinion." *No matter how misguided it might be!*

He didn't respond right away. He rocked on his heels and simply looked at her, a slight frown puckering his brow. Then, to her surprise, he reached out, traced his forefinger over her jaw and said gently, "It's been a long day, hasn't it?"

"Yes," she half muttered, melting beneath his touch. How badly she wanted to turn her head and trap his hand; to kiss it and in so doing turn his casual gesture of kindness into something close and intimate and unforgettable.

"Then let's put Tommy back under the covers and get some rest. He's sleeping quite peacefully now, see?"

So he was. When Pierce lifted him from her shoulder, she saw that his long blond lashes lay on his cheek and he was breathing evenly again.

Carefully, Pierce placed the child's head on the pillow and tucked his Winnie the Pooh quilt around him. Then, straightening, he held out his hand and pulled Nicole to her feet.

His clasp was warm and strong, the kind a woman could depend on. Against her better judgment she let her hand linger in his, cherishing the moment and expecting that he would end it by withdrawing from her. But he didn't. Instead, he wove his fingers between hers, walked her out into the upstairs hall and tugged her around to face him.

Behind him, the door to her suite stood open, spilling a runway of lamplight over the polished floorboards and beckoning her to safety. Blindly, she went to move past him, knowing that the sooner she left Pierce Warner, the farther removed she'd be from acting on the crazy impulses welling within her.

"Nicole?" His hand slid to her arm, halting her escape.

"Hmm?" She did not—dare not—look at him.

"Everything's all right, isn't it? Between us, I mean?"

If only! "Uh-huh."

"If it isn't, I wish you'd tell me."

Was the way he was stroking her wrist an attempt on his part to mesmerize her into unwise confession, the adult equivalent to patting a baby on the back to rid it of indigestion, or was he simply trying to drive her wild? Did he really want her to spit out the appalling truth: that her emotions where he was concerned were getting away from her; that she was eaten alive with jealousy whenever she thought of Louise Trent in his arms; that she was afraid she might be falling in love with him?

She uttered a sound midway between a laugh and a sob. Heavenly days, how incredibly clichéd the whole situation was! "Everything's fine," she choked, wrestling to control herself.

"I hope so."

Did he realize that they were standing much too close? Was that what caused his voice to jolt unevenly, the way a car might if it hit a patch of gravel on an otherwise smooth road? But if that were the case, why didn't he let go of her, step back, put some space between them? Why, instead, did he slide his palms inside the wide sleeves of her dressing gown, cup her elbows and propel her toward him?

"Because," he went on, in the same husky murmur, "I don't know how I'd manage without you, Nicole. You haven't been here very long, but already you've made yourself..."

"Useful?" she croaked, aware that the distant trembling deep within her was merely the precursor of much greater upheaval should all this continue. Yet everything conspired against her: the middle-of-the-night silence which amplified even her heartbeat into a clamor, the sanction of the shadows lurking around them, the atmosphere itself which hummed with vibrant tension.

"Not exactly," he said, bringing just enough pressure to bear on her elbows to inch her even nearer. "Indispensable is more the word I'd use."

The description floated between them, preposterously erotic. Nothing he might have said instead—no hushed endearment, no muttered comment on her face or figure—could have conveyed more clearly that somehow, in the space of a nanosecond, their association had shifted to assume a different focus.

He's going to kiss me! she thought, her brain at last connecting with the awareness suffusing her body.

Relentlessly, he steered her closer, introducing her to his contours and textures a little at a time. She felt the long, lean muscles of his thighs nudge against her, followed by the more aggressive thrust of his hips. She saw the broad wedge of his shoulder eclipse the light behind him, explored with her fingertips the slubbed weave of his jacket, shivered at the slight abrasion of his jaw against her cheek. His hands spanned her waist, his chest crushed her breasts.

She thought that her heart would leap free of her rib cage and fasten itself to his, matching thunderous beat for thunderous beat. She thought that her lungs might explode, that her entire body would collapse, softened beyond endurance by the heat shimmering between them.

His mouth brushed over hers, so softly seductive that

she thought she'd die from the sheer sweetness of it. Closing her eyes, she breathed in the scent of him. He smelled of Oregon pines bathed in moonlight. Of sea breezes and sandalwood...and very faintly of jasmine and musk.

He smelled of Louise Trent!

Abruptly, Nicole jerked back, braced her palms against his chest and thrust him away from her. "How dare you!" she snapped.

He straightened, the smoky haze of passion clearing from his eyes like mist lifting from a morning sky and leaving him looking startled, as though he hadn't the first clue how he'd come to be caught in such a compromising situation.

"Forgive me, Nicole." He gave just enough of a shrug for the dangling end of his tie to sway from his jacket pocket in taunting reminder of where and how he'd spent the earlier part of the evening. "That was out of line."

"Yes," she said. "It was."

"It won't happen again."

No, sadly it wouldn't. By tomorrow, he'd wonder what sort of mental aberration had tempted him to spare her a second glance, let alone kiss her. "It had better not," she said.

He didn't join them for breakfast the next morning, a rare omission made even more unusual by the fact that it was Sunday.

"He ate earlier," Janet said, when Nicole asked. "Mentioned something about having a load of paperwork to catch up on before tomorrow and said he didn't want to be disturbed."

But when he didn't show up for lunch, either, opting instead for a sandwich at his desk in the library, Nicole was forced to assume that he was deliberately avoiding her, a theory made all the more credible when he suddenly appeared in the garden around three in the afternoon and relieved her of her duties for the rest of the day.

"You've taken hardly any time off," he said, not quite meeting her eye. "Go see your relatives, or something. You did say they were the chief reason you chose to move here, didn't you?"

Alarm raced through her at that. What if he asked her where her relatives lived, or worse, their names? In weaving her web of lies, this had been one eventuality she'd neglected to consider. "Perhaps I will," she said, anxious to make her escape before any such awkward questions arose.

"Stay away overnight, if you like. As long as you're back before I leave for work in the morning, I can manage Tom on my own."

Stay where? She had no other address, not this side of the Rockies at any rate. Without Tommy to anchor her, she was little better than one of the homeless people she'd seen sleeping on park benches in downtown Morningside.

"I'll be back long before then," she said, bending down to give her nephew a hug. "'Bye, sweetheart. See you in the morning."

"No!" Tommy protested, clinging to her knees. "I want to come with you."

"Nicole's off duty for the next little while, Tom, so it's going to be just us men. Let her go, sport. She deserves a little playtime, just like the rest of us."

Pierce spoke kindly enough, but Tommy was not disposed to cooperate. "No!" he wailed, flinging himself down on the lawn in a rare display of temper. "I don't like you. I like Nicole."

Pierce jerked his head toward the house. "Just leave," he told her. "I'll deal with this."

"I hate leaving him when he's this upset."

"And I hate having to argue with you when I've already got my hands full trying to cope with him," he snapped.

Still, she hesitated, heartsick as Tommy's howls escalated.

"*Go!*" Pierce blasted the order at her, his eyes stormy.

I have nowhere to go, she wanted to yell back. Everything I care about is right here, with you and Tommy.

But, of course, she couldn't say that, any more than she could lean against those strong masculine shoulders and sob out the truth, and expect him to say, "It's all right. I understand. Together we'll work things out, we'll make them better."

All she could do was make her way inside, with Tommy's shrieks following her, and be grateful that, by the time she'd reached her suite, the garden was silent again.

Carefully lifting the corner of the window shade, she peeked out. Pierce and Tommy sat facing each other on the grass. Pierce was talking and Tommy appeared to be listening. She should have been relieved. Instead, she felt left out.

"Better watch it, Nicole," she muttered, letting the shade fall into place and going through to her bedroom. "You're in trouble enough already, with the deception you're practicing. Put a halt to this romantic nonsense now, before everything blows up in your face."

Every weekend during the summer months, an open-air market was held in Morningside's Central Park, a huge area encompassing a pier, the beach and a wide grassy expanse shaded by poplars. Everyone, from permanent residents to tourists, flocked to the site and everything, from hand-crafted silver jewelry to Mexican pottery to dust-laden trash posing as antiques, could be found under the striped awnings stretched over the stalls.

Nicole gravitated toward that market like a flower reaching out to the sun. Pierce had been right to insist she take some time off. She needed to be with people—

happy anonymous people with whom she didn't have always to be on guard.

The voices, the music, the jostle of bodies, reminded her that there was a world beyond Pierce's house; that grief eventually faded to make room for the joy of living. It had been so long since she'd laughed or danced or just had fun. For all that she adored being with Tommy, the specter of her deceit followed her everywhere at the house, and underlying it, the tragic reason for her lies. It felt good to forget all that for a little while, to be just another tourist enjoying the afternoon.

She wandered among the stalls, came across a rack of T-shirt dresses, found one in bright coral that she tried on in a fitting room made of two curtains strung across a wire in the corner of the canvas booth and a mirror suspended from a coat hanger. Pleased with how the dress looked on her, she bought it and another in a deep peacock blue.

Down the next aisle, she discovered a vinyl bibbed apron decorated with a Renoir print. Janet would surely love it—and the battery-operated nutmeg grater without which, the salesman assured Nicole, no kitchen was complete.

The toy displays she avoided. The temptation to lavish gifts on Tommy was simply too great and too risky. Aunts could indulge their nephews; nannies were supposed to know better. Instead, she bought him a striped papier-mâché fish, something inexpensive, colorful and amusing for his room.

As the sun slipped behind the trees, hunger pangs drove her toward the restaurant at the end of the pier. Unfortunately, other people had the same idea. "It'll be about ten minutes before I can give you a table," the hostess informed her, "but you can enjoy a drink in the lounge while you're waiting, if you like."

She didn't normally frequent bars, and she seldom drank alone, but the carnival atmosphere was contagious. "Why not?" she said, and ordered a wine spritzer.

The lounge was cool and spacious, with lots of indoor greenery and full-length windows that looked over the water. The cane swivel chairs were deep and comfortable, the music low and soothing.

After the heat of the market, it was pleasant to relax in the privacy offered by the screen of plants beside her table; to slip off her sandals, stretch out her legs, sip her drink and enjoy the music. She'd treat herself to a good dinner then, after dusk had fallen, she'd sneak back to the house and spend the night in her own bed, in her own room, with Pierce being none the wiser.

As close to contentment as she'd been since the day she'd arrived in Morningside, she leaned her head against the high back of her chair and let herself be hypnotized by the endless roll of the tide.

She might have dozed off—heaven knew, she'd hardly slept well the night before—had a new arrival not tripped over her feet.

"Please excuse me!" a voice exclaimed and then, inexplicably, shrieked softly, "Oh!"

Bolting upright in her chair, Nicole found herself confronting a woman whose eyes were dark holes of shock in her pale face. Her hand was pressed to her mouth and the bag she'd been carrying lay on the floor, its contents spilling over at her feet.

The stranger stared at Nicole; Nicole stared at the stranger. And for a second, time tripped over itself as though uncertain whether to run forward or backward. Then the woman recovered, albeit shakily.

Fingers splayed, her hand dropped to her heart. "Oh!" she said weakly, then again, "Oh! I do apologize! For a moment, I thought you were someone else— a very dear friend of mine...just something in your face as you were sleeping. I'm so sorry to have wakened you."

"I wasn't sleeping," Nicole said with a smile. "I was just resting my eyes. And I'm sorry I'm not the person you were expecting to see."

"You hardly could be. My friend..." The woman swallowed, bent to retrieve the items from her bag, and glanced again at Nicole. "Well, Arlene died in a car accident. Just over three months ago."

Nicole's smile froze into horror.

Misunderstanding, the woman rose swiftly to her feet and dropped into the chair next to Nicole's. "I'm sorry, I didn't mean that to sound so ghoulish. I was just taken aback, that's all, and for a moment, I almost forgot that...." She hunched her shoulders apologetically. "You must think I'm nuts."

"No." Nicole said woodenly. "Not at all. You obviously miss your friend very much." *Your friend, whose name was Arlene and who, for a second, you thought looked just a bit like me!*

She wished with all her heart that she could confide in this woman, that they could console each other. Wished she could have learned more about the sister she'd come so close to finding again.

The woman sighed and leaned back in the chair. "She was like a sister to me."

But she wasn't your sister; she was mine! "I'm so sorry."

The woman slewed her glance sideways to where Nicole perched on the edge of her seat, and smiled. "Do you realize how many times we keep saying that?"

"What?"

"That we're sorry. We must have repeated it about twenty times in the last five minutes."

Nicole looked away, out to where the blue-green sea heaved and rolled toward the shore. "Sometimes, they're the only words that fit."

"Yes. And sometimes, there aren't any words at all."

"I know."

"May I buy you another drink?" The woman gestured to where the wine spritzer had splashed over the table. "I could use one myself and I'm afraid you've lost most of yours."

"Thank you, but no." She had to escape, quickly before her composure shattered. Who would have expected she'd run into a friend of Arlene's? And worse, if this woman had noticed the resemblance, who else might? "I really must be going."

"Well then, thank you for not making me feel like a complete fool. And for what it's worth, you don't really look like Arlene at all. She was blond and you...well, you're dark. I don't know what it was that made me see a resemblance..." She regarded Nicole searchingly. "Perhaps it's the mouth. She had a lovely smile, too."

The panic rose to choke Nicole again. "I've changed my mind," she said, when the hostess suddenly appeared to tell her her table was ready. "I'm afraid I can't stay, after all."

"Good bye," Arlene's friend called after her, as she scooped up her parcels and fled toward the exit. "Perhaps we'll see each other again sometime."

Oh, she hoped not. She really hoped not!

CHAPTER FOUR

SHE wasn't thinking clearly as she reentered the market. Her only objective was to reach her car, which she'd left at the other end of the park, and race away from the scene of such near disaster.

A yelp stopped her in her tracks. Just ahead, she saw a puppy cringing under the table to which it was tied by a length of rope. A passing tourist had stepped on one of its front paws which it held up piteously.

Nicole made two mistakes then.

The first was merely foolish. She stopped and bent down to console the puppy. It was all legs and tail, and soft, warm fur the color of honey.

The second—entering into conversation with its stony-hearted owner—was fatal. A man stepped down from the bed of a pickup parked next to the stall. "You interested, lady? She's going cheap."

It was then that Nicole noticed the sign propped on a chair. FOR SALE 10 WEEK OLD GOLDEN RETRIEVER NO PAPERS.

The puppy had the saddest eyes she'd ever seen.

Why didn't she just shake her head and keep going? Why did she make it impossible to walk away from the pathetic bundle of fur by picking it up and allowing it to burrow into her neck? Why in the name of everything sane and sensible did she say, "She's adorable. How can you bear to part with her?"

"'Cause I got enough mouths to feed." The man jerked his head at the woman trailing behind him with a child slung across one hip and another hanging on her skirt. "Either I sell the mutt or else..." He made a slashing motion across his throat with one grimy finger.

The dog whimpered and lifted a paw to Nicole, one lost soul reaching out to another.

The idea—outrageous and presumptuous though it was—took shape and refused to go ignored. Pierce had suggested getting a dog for Tommy; here was a dog in desperate need of a home. That Nicole also needed something of her own to love, something that didn't belong primarily to someone else, was a minor consideration.

I can't do this, she thought. *I don't have the right.*

"I'll take her," she said, closing her mind to the probable repercussions of such a decision. At the very worst, she'd have to ship the poor little scrap home to her parents. At best, she now had good reason to return to the house that night.

It was a pretty paltry best. All the way back she rehearsed what she'd say. *I saved its life, Pierce,* seemed a reasonable beginning. But when she pulled her car into the third garage, she saw that although Louise's dark red Taurus was parked under the trees, Pierce's black Mercury Marquis was missing, which must mean they'd left Janet to baby-sit and gone out somewhere for dinner. Which was fine with Nicole; it bought her extra time to think up a more persuasive argument.

Grateful for the reprieve, she hurried to the kitchen.

"He took Tommy *and* Miss Trent out for the afternoon," Janet informed her, relieving her of her smaller packages. "Gracious me, Nicole, what've you got in there?"

"I guess you could call it an impulse buy." Nicole lifted the puppy out of the cardboard box in which she'd shipped her home and waited apprehensively for Janet's reaction.

Janet, who was, above all else, a thoroughly down-to-earth woman, clasped her hands and declared, "It's a dog and scarcely old enough to do without its mother's milk. Put it out on the back lawn quick, before it wets on my clean floor, and I'll fix it something for supper."

"Do you think Pierce will let me keep her?" Nicole asked a little later, as they watched the puppy snuffle her way through a bowl of warm cereal.

"You mean, the Commander doesn't—? Don't tell me...!" For once at a loss, Janet look scandalized.

Nicole nodded miserably, the consequences of her actions at last coming home to roost. "I did this without his permission."

"Gracious me, Nicole!" Janet exclaimed again. "How could you?"

"I had no choice. The man who sold her to me was going to have the poor thing put down if he didn't find a buyer."

"Talk about one being born every minute!" Janet rolled her eyes scornfully. "You realize he likely has ten more where this one came from? Probably steals them, if truth be known. And that he'll be there again next weekend, playing the same old tune?"

"No," Nicole said faintly. "I didn't realize that. And if it's all the same to you, I'd just as soon not dwell on the fact, or I might find myself running a kennel before much longer."

Just then, a beam of light swept over the darkened shrubbery outside the kitchen windows. "Right now, you've bigger problems," Janet predicted, eyeing the puppy which had curled into a warm ball and gone to sleep at Nicole's feet. "The Commander just drove up and if I were you, I'd wait until tomorrow to spring this little surprise on him. It's my guess that after an afternoon with Tommy *and* Miss Louise, he'll not be in the best of moods."

"You're right." Nicole picked up the puppy, popped her back into her box, and thrust the whole works into Janet's arms. "Help me out, Janet. Just for tonight, keep her here in the kitchen. She can't get into much trouble confined to this box."

"Let us hope not," Janet sniffed. "What's its name, by the way?"

Nicole shrugged helplessly and touched a finger to the soft pale fur. "Honey, maybe? Or Peaches? I don't know. I haven't really thought about it much."

"You haven't been thinking at all today, if you ask me," Janet said darkly. "Stick the thing under the table out of sight and pray the Commander doesn't decide to come in here for a late night snack or we're both for the high jump."

Pierce carried Tom up to the nursery, peeled off his filthy clothes, and dunked him in a warm bath. Heaven knew the boy needed it. He was covered in ketchup, ice cream and a lot of other unmentionable stuff.

By the time he was clean again, he was practically asleep on his feet and Pierce needed a bath himself. It seemed a fitting way to erase the memories of what had turned out to be a generally disastrous day.

Tom had never really recovered from Nicole's leaving, and it hadn't done a whole lot for Pierce's ego that the kid found him such a poor substitute for the nanny.

He'd decided taking the boy out for the afternoon would make up for things, and when Louise had shown up unexpectedly, that inviting her along on the jaunt might help. If anything, it had made matters worse.

"That child is spoiled," she had declared when, at Tom's admittedly whiny insistence, they'd stopped for cold drinks within fifteen minutes of leaving the house. "And it's mostly thanks to that nanny you hired, Pierce."

"I thought you approved of her," Pierce had said.

Louise had removed herself a safe distance from Tom's efforts to squirt orange soda out of his straw. "That was before I realized what a mess she'd make of the job."

"I think she's doing rather well. Tom seems to be adjusting to the change."

He spoke mildly enough—no reason to take his frustration out on Louise, after all—but she must have realized he was operating on rather a short fuse because when she spoke again, a more conciliatory note softened her voice. "Sweets, I'm not criticizing you. I know you're doing your best and for that I love you."

I love you. The silence following those three words twanged with expectant tension—what was known as a pregnant pause, he supposed, and one he knew he was expected to end, just as he knew what it was he was expected to end it with. Trouble was, he couldn't quite bring himself to echo the sentiment.

Instead, he'd mopped up the mess Tom had made and suggested they drive down the coast to Cleves where there was an amusement park. Louise had stared out of the car window the entire time, the angle of her head and tilt of her shoulder proclaiming her disappointment in him.

In a way, he hadn't blamed her. They'd been dating for five months and without it ever becoming an item of discussion, their pairing had taken on a definition of permanence. In time, he supposed they'd get married, have children—or, more accurately, have *more* children, since, for all intents and purposes, Tom was now his son. But Jim and Arlene's dying had put everything on hold for a while. He'd assumed Louise understood that.

Perhaps he'd assumed too much on more than one front. Hiring Nicole, for example, had seemed like a good idea, a way to ease Tom into this new, unsettling phase of his life. Why, just when things were finally getting squared away, had she become a complication he didn't need?

That business last night, when he'd kissed her.... Hell, just thinking about it had him breaking out in a sweat!

The amusement park had gone over pretty well, at least from Tom's point of view. He rode the carousel, the children's Ferris wheel and the bumper cars, squealing happily throughout.

Louise hadn't said much—it wasn't the best place for conversation—but she'd been a good sport, waiting around in her high heels and putting up with all the noise. In fact, the only time she'd really opened her mouth had been when Tom had begged to go on the roller coaster.

"You're crazy to give in to him on that, Pierce," she'd said. "He'll get sick, being thrown around like that."

Pierce hadn't listened. He'd been too glad that Tom wasn't howling or scowling or both. "He'll be fine, he's got sailing in his blood," he'd bragged, certain that nothing an amusement park offered could equal the motion of a ship under heavy seas. "In fact, why don't you come on with us?"

But she'd dug her high heels in at that and flatly refused. "He's not going to throw up on me!"

Tom had been a trouper, shrieking with terrified delight and clinging to his uncle in a way that more than made up for his earlier rejection. A guy could get used to this parenting thing, Pierce had decided.

By the time they left the park and headed home though, the sun was setting and Tom was fading just about as fast, whining about being hungry and thirsty and hot, so they'd stopped for dinner at a fast-food joint on the beach midway between Morningside and Cleves.

He and Tom had gone for the whole works—burgers, fries and chocolate milk shakes—but Louise had wanted only a salad. That had been when he'd realized she'd been pretty quiet for a long time, which wasn't like her.

"Hey," he'd said, wondering if she'd had too much sun. "Is everything okay?"

She'd sort of sighed, and her face had a pinched look to it. "I don't know," she'd said. "You tell me."

He'd stared at her, baffled, then been distracted by Tom who'd slopped enough ketchup on his food to keep an army supplied for a month.

"I mean," she'd gone on, sounding decidedly peeved, "are you even aware that I'm here?"

He honestly hadn't known what she was talking about.

Hadn't he just addressed a question to her? "Well, of course you're here," he'd said, more mystified than ever.

"But does it really mean anything to you, Pierce? Or would any other woman do just as well? Nanny Nicole, for instance? Am I just a convenient body when you're in the mood for a little healthy sex—not that you have been for weeks now!"

"Don't talk like that," he'd muttered, glancing at Tom. "There are little ears around."

She'd slapped her fork down and her eyes had sparkled with tears. "That's precisely what I mean! Ever since that little…*boy* moved in, you've scarcely given me the time of day."

He hadn't liked the way she'd made "boy" sound like a three-letter expletive. But more than that, he hadn't liked the quiver in her voice. "Don't start crying," he'd begged, wondering how in hell a simple question like "Is everything okay?" could turn so suddenly into an emotional blood-letting. "Honestly, Louise, if that's the impression I've given you, I'm sorry."

He'd shrugged helplessly. "I thought you understood the way things have to be now. I can't be the swinging bachelor I was when we met. I've got responsibilities and they're going to be around for a long time."

"I know."

"If it's all too much for you and you'd be happier seeing other men—"

"No," she'd whimpered, her eyes shining like jewels. He'd always heard that women were supposed to look a mess when they cried; that their noses turned red and the whites of their eyes pink. But Louise looked beautiful. "Oh, Pierce, that's not what I want at all."

"Well, good," he'd said, keeping an eye on Tom who'd decided that stuffing French fries into his milk shake was a better idea than eating them. "As long as you understand that I can't turn my back on Tom."

"Sweets," she'd murmured, dabbing at her eyes, "I'd

never ask you to do that. I think it's wonderful, the way you've taken over for his father. Thomas is an adorable child. As for that unfortunate remark I made about Nicole—''

He didn't want to talk about Nicole, not to Louise. "Forget it," he said. "I have."

"That's good. But, sweetness, Thomas does need a firm hand and I frankly believe Nicole is too permissive. It's not good for a boy to be mollycoddled, Pierce."

"I guess not."

Their waitress had come by then to clear away their plates. "How would you like ice cream for dessert, hon?" she'd asked Tom.

"Oh, boy!" he'd beamed, then just to make sure she'd follow through on the offer, added without being prompted, "Please."

"It's not every day I take him out for treats," Pierce had said defensively, seeing Louise about to object.

She'd pursed her lips in a tight smile. "Whatever you think is best, Pierce."

"It'll give him something to do while we have coffee."

"Of course. Make mine strong," she'd added to the waitress.

Pierce had slung his arm around the back of her chair and squeezed her shoulder. "If the weather stays fine, we should do something special this weekend. Got any ideas?"

Without meaning to, he'd managed to put his foot in things again. "Don't tell me you've forgotten!" she wailed. "Oh, Pierce, how could you, after all the trouble I've gone to?"

"For what?" he'd said, firmly believing that a man gained nothing from trying to lie his way out of trouble.

"Why, your housewarming party next Saturday, of course!"

"I had forgotten. I'm sorry. But couldn't it wait?"

He'd glanced meaningfully at Tom. "I mean, it hasn't been so long since—"

"Life goes on, sweetie, and in Thomas' case, the sooner, the better, wouldn't you say?"

He'd shrugged. "Maybe. I guess so."

"It isn't as if you don't have hired help. Between Nicole and Janet, surely one small, sweet boy isn't going to present a problem?"

That wasn't exactly what Pierce had meant, but the small sweet boy in question chose that moment to offer a diversion all of his own making. Wielding his spoon with deadly aim, he landed a blob of melted chocolate ice cream smack in the middle of Louise's white linen skirt.

After that, Pierce hadn't thought the evening could get any worse.

He'd been wrong. They'd been only halfway home when he'd had to stop the car while Tom threw up at the side of the road. Louise hadn't said a word. Instead she'd given Pierce a lesson on how silence could indeed speak louder than words.

When they'd finally arrived back at the house, he'd invited her in for a nightcap. "No thanks," she'd said shortly. "Vomity children make me nervous."

Nervous? That little incident? Hell, it was nothing to some of the sights he'd seen at sea! But the tension sparking between them as she'd thanked him for "*such* a lovely day" was downright intimidating. Small wonder that, by the time she'd hopped into her car and sped off, he was ready to kick back with a good stiff drink.

Toweling off his hair, he strolled to the window and looked out. The night was clear and warm, with a faint breeze coming in over the water. Directly below, the pool shone translucently in the otherwise dark garden, too inviting to resist.

Perhaps a few laps would iron out the kinks to which his spine was now so prone. The fresh air might sweeten his mood. And the Scotch he intended to consume right after might give him just enough of a buzz that he'd see the future as somewhat rosier than it now appeared.

Within five minutes he stood poised on the diving board. Taking a deep, relaxing breath, he knifed into the water. It closed around him, smooth and warm as a woman's arms, but so much less complicated or demanding.

Twenty-five laps later, he felt like a new man. Rolling over, he began a lazy back crawl. The ocean whispered below the cliff. Overhead, Ursa Minor shone clear and bright.

In a perfect world, he'd have been in command of his own ship, somewhere in the Persian Gulf most likely. Jim and Arlene would be alive and Tom would have both his parents, as well as an uncle who sent him exotic gifts from foreign parts. And women would be something to look forward to at the next port of call.

Folding his arms behind his head and floating lazily, Pierce stared up at the stars and decided that if what he had instead didn't quite measure up to the same thing, it was still pretty damned nice. Peaceful, calm, orderly, with Tom asleep in his bed and all more or less right with the world.

Except for the dog howling in a neighbor's house....

Except for the fact that the nearest house lay half a block away and what he heard was closer. Much closer.

Nicole had waited until Pierce had put Tommy to bed and the house had sunk back into silence before she'd turned on the lights in her own suite and gone about making an early night of it herself. The day had been exhausting on a number of levels.

Then, just as she emerged from a long, luxurious bath, she heard a sound. Her first thought was that Tommy was having another nightmare. Snatching up her bathrobe and pulling it on, she stole to his door. But when she peeked in, she found him spread-eagled on his bed and snoring.

She was backing away when the noise came again, a lonely, pathetic wail, followed by a high-pitched little bark. Spinning around, Nicole stared down the hall, half expecting to see the puppy bounding up the stairs in search of her.

Although a crack of light showed underneath, the door to Pierce's room remained closed. Paralyzed, she waited for him to wrench it open and demand an explanation. When a full thirty seconds passed with nothing but the magnified sound of her heart disturbing the silence, she relaxed and began a stealthy return to her own suite.

Before she was even halfway home, the barking began again, more frenzied and infinitely louder than before. Far from being so exhausted that it wanted nothing but to be left to sleep in peace, the puppy seemed determined to arouse the entire household. Scuttling past Pierce's door, Nicole fled down the stairs and along the passage to the kitchen.

The puppy's box lay tipped over on its side with the old towel which Janet had provided for temporary bedding trailing across the floor. But of the dog itself there was no sign. The only living creature in the kitchen was a pseudo-nanny whose rash actions of the previous afternoon assumed an even more foolhardy aspect by the dim gloom of night.

Puppies chewed things. Until they were house-broken, they left little deposits anyplace the urge took them. And even something as small as a ten-week-old retriever could push open the swing door that led from the kitchen to the main body of the house.

Thinking of the havoc that could be wreaked by tiny teeth on the fine mahogany furniture in the living room, of the souvenirs that might be left behind on the rare Aubusson carpet in the dining room, not to mention the devastation that could be visited on Pierce's beloved library, made Nicole's blood run cold.

"Honey?" she whispered, pushing open the swinging door and peering down the corridor in the desperate hope that she'd find the errant creature before someone else did. "Peaches? Come out, come out, wherever you are, you little monkey. You're going to get me keelhauled if our high and mighty Commander is disturbed."

"We don't do that anymore, Nicole," a voice from the other side of the room informed her. "We have other ways of meting out punishment."

Swallowing a tiny shriek, Nicole whirled around. Pierce stood framed in the doorway leading out to the deck beyond the kitchen, the fine glaze of water on his skin and the towel tucked around his waist attesting to where he'd come from. For once, however, his splendid physique failed to capture her attention.

"Oh, Honey-Peaches!" she wheezed, rushing toward the squirming bundle he held in the crook of one arm. "There you are!"

Pierce lofted the puppy out of reach and fended Nicole off with his other hand. "Honey-Peaches?" he inquired, with malicious amusement. "A second ago, I was your 'high and mighty Commander.' What's brought about such a fond, not to mention excessive, change of heart?"

"Don't be ridiculous," she said, consigning good manners to perdition along with self-preservation and common sense. "I was referring to the dog."

"Dog?" he echoed, batting his water-soaked eyelashes in a parody of bewilderment. "You must be mistaken. We don't own a dog."

"We do now," she said boldly, since the evidence was irrefutable. "I bought her this afternoon at the market in the park. She's a Golden Retriever cross and—"

"She's about as much Golden Retriever as I am French poodle," he said. "As for the name—it's only slightly less ridiculous than your assuming I wouldn't notice there was another mouth to feed." He regarded her severely. "You don't have a very high opinion of my intelligence, do you, Nicole?"

"No," she began, then rapidly amended the statement before she alienated him completely. "I mean, no, that's not true. I have tremendous respect for you, in every possible way, and I'm very sorry if it seems that I've taken advantage of you by bringing a dog into your home without your express permission.''

"Isn't that exactly what you've done?''

She tilted one shoulder apologetically. "Yes. But I didn't feel I had any other choice.''

"Really? You rescued the dog from a swift and unhappy end, did you?''

"Yes,'' she said again, taking comfort from the fact that, whether or not he realized it, he was caressing Honey-Peaches' ears gently. "The man who owned her said he was going to have her put down if he didn't find a home for her today. And you did say, Pierce, that you thought a dog might be a good idea for Tommy.''

"Remind me not to ruminate out loud in front of you again,'' he replied dryly. "It's a hazardous undertaking.''

"Yes,'' she said demurely. "May we keep her, Pierce?''

He expelled a long-suffering sigh and with his free hand hitched the towel more securely around his hips. The gesture, along with the amount of tanned flesh on view, made her wonder if he was wearing anything else.

He spoke again, the sound of his voice causing her to start guiltily. "I was just about to unwind with a quiet drink by the pool. I figured I'd earned it, considering the afternoon I've just put in.''

"You didn't have a good time with Tommy?''

"It was hell. Oh, he was okay, I suppose, but the rest of it…let's just say I didn't need this mutt baying at the top of its lungs and disturbing the peace to top things off. This isn't a good time to appeal to my better nature, Nicole.''

If you even have one, she thought, as Honey-Peaches whimpered and burrowed deeper into the protection of Pierce's hold. How could anyone remain impervious to such a helpless little creature?

"Well, if that's asking too much, at least will you agree to keep her here until I can make other arrangements?"

"I didn't say it was too much. I said this wasn't the best time to arrive at any decisions, nor the best place, either, come to that." He glanced meaningfully at the puddle gathering around his feet. "I'm dripping water all over Janet's clean floor and this dog's probably going to add to the mess any moment now. If you insist on discussing the matter, let's do it outside. In fact, come down to the pool with me and we'll try to arrive at a compromise."

"What sort of compromise?" she asked warily.

"Join me in a drink and I'll agree to look at the pros and cons of keeping her. A little adult conversation might dispose me to view the matter more charitably."

Nicole thought it sounded more like blackmail than compromise, but she hardly felt she was in a position to argue the point.

"I'll open a bottle of wine," he added persuasively. "I know you don't care for Scotch."

"Isn't it a bit late to be outside?"

"Half-past nine is scarcely late."

"I was talking about the temperature. It'll be too cold."

"It's seventy-five degrees out there. The patio bricks are still warm from the sun." He hoisted Honey-Peaches onto the broad palm of his hand so that her front legs dangled between his fingers, and smiled winningly. "What's with all the excuses, Nicole? Why are you so reluctant to give a few more minutes of your precious time to helping me decide what to do about this benighted creature that you've brought into my home?"

Nicole knew why. Wine, moonlight and Pierce Warner at his most charming were about as safe a combination as gasoline and fire, no matter what the reason.

"I'm not making excuses," she said.

"Really? That's what it sounds like to me. In fact, if

I didn't know better, I'd say you're afraid to be alone in the dark with me.''

Ahh! She caught the exclamation just in time and swallowed it. ''That's absurd!''

''Then you'll join me?''

''If you insist.''

''I do.'' Although the winning smile didn't slip an inch, there was no mistaking his peremptory tone. ''Go change into your swimsuit and be quick about it.''

She resisted the urge to click her heels together and salute, or better yet, remind him he was no longer in the Navy and that it was customary among polite civilians to say ''please'' and ''thank you'' occasionally. Under the circumstances, however, it seemed politic to do neither. The puppy's fate still hung too much in the balance. ''All right.''

''Bring the baby monitor,'' he said, still in Commander mode, ''just in case Tom wakes up, though I can't imagine he will after the day he's had.''

''What about...?'' Nicole gestured at Honey-Peaches who continued to dangle from the palm of Pierce's hand.

''I'll bring the mutt down to the pool. No point in leaving it here to howl and raise the whole neighborhood.'' He inclined his head toward the door behind her. ''Hop to it, Nicole. Time's a-wasting and I don't like the way your protégée is squirming around.''

She wasn't sure what prompted her to choose a swimsuit which she'd owned in her other life but had rejected as being too risqué for a nanny to wear, with its plunging neckline and high-cut legs. The need to convince herself that she was still in charge of her own life, despite his attempts to run it for her? The urge to test her susceptibility to him—or his to her? Certainly, for a woman who, just minutes before, had experienced a profound reluctance to play with fire, it was a rash decision, a fact borne home to her the moment she dropped her cover-up on one of the two chaises Pierce had drawn up beside a small glass-topped table bearing a wine cooler and two liqueur glasses.

"That's new," he said, pausing in the act of uncorking a small bottle to run an appraising eye over the swimsuit.

"No. I've had it for ages."

His gaze settled on her shoulders, slid to her waist, somehow bypassing the bits in between as if they were too obscene to merit attention, and coming to rest midway between her knees and her hips. "It's not like the one you usually wear."

There was nothing overtly critical in the observation but his glance, along with something in his tone, left her feeling indecently exposed. As if to compound the matter, the moon chose that moment to swim out from behind the trees and bathe her in a glare so brightly revealing that she almost cringed.

Scooping Honey-Peaches from her spot in the middle of one of the chaises, Nicole clutched her to her bosom, thereby covering that portion of her anatomy Pierce seemed to find most offensive. Annoyed as much with herself as with Pierce, she said defiantly, "No, it's not. What would be the point in always buying the same thing?"

He cleared his throat, obviously taken aback by such aggression. "No point, I guess. It's just such a…change. I always think of you as more…"

"Dowdy?" she suggested, when he clearly couldn't come up with a word that fit his idea of how a properly-attired nanny should look.

"Conservative," he said. "You never struck me as the flamboyant type."

"Sorry if I've disappointed you," she said, wondering if he'd ever noticed that Louise Trent's hemlines were practically on speaking terms with her waist.

"I didn't say you had. Surprised me, perhaps. You were the one, after all, who seemed to prefer more…"

He cleared his throat again and offered her a glass containing a pale gold liquid. "More sedate swimwear."

She gripped Honey-Peaches even tighter. "I'm allowed to change my mind, and so, apparently, are you. That isn't wine you're pouring."

"It's ice wine, and very pleasant—a sort of cross between a liqueur and—"

"I know what it is," she snapped, resenting his assumption that her palate was as callow as her taste in bathing attire.

He took a mouthful of the wine. "You're full of surprises tonight, aren't you?"

"No," she said, tired suddenly, of sparring with him and wishing she could abandon the role she'd elected to play and simply be herself. "I guess, like you, I've just had a long day."

"All the more reason to relax now, then." Taking her untouched glass and returning it with his on the table, he pried Honey-Peaches away from her. "Leave the mutt to sleep on the chaise before you strangle it, Nicole, and come for a swim with me."

She'd swum with him before. More accurately, she'd been in the pool with him before, often. So why did her heart lurch violently and her pulse suddenly race? What was it that made swimming with him now, with only the moon for company, so much more dangerous and exciting?

She knew why. Before, Tommy had always been with them, a reminder of why she was involved in this bizarre and tragic charade whose rules only she fully understood. Tonight, there was nothing to come between her and Pierce; no pretense, no predetermined rules, not even the repressive black maillot which made her look more like a college sophomore than a woman in her prime.

"Come," he said again, his voice low and hypnotic.

Metaphorically, those innocent turquoise waters were infested with sharks bent on destroying her. Still, she obeyed him.

Wordlessly, she placed Honey-Peaches on the chaise and followed, trancelike, as he led her down the steps at the shallow end of the pool. When their feet touched bottom, he backed into deeper water and drew her after him.

Too soon she was out of her depth but still he didn't release her. Instead, he pulled her toward him so that her legs tangled with his. The sharks circled closer. "See?" he murmured huskily. "This isn't so bad, is it?"

Not bad, perhaps, but foolish.

And dangerous. Definitely dangerous!

And heaven.

He tugged her into the middle of the pool. Slid his arms around her waist and closed the last tiny gap between them. There was little doubt in her mind that he was going to kiss her, and none at all that she was going to let him.

And that was the most dangerous, foolish, heavenly thing of all.

CHAPTER FIVE

Ever since that other, too-brief exchange in the upstairs hall, she'd dreamed about his kissing her again. But nothing could have prepared her for the reality of it. Reality? Magic was a more apt description, a slow-spreading enchantment that began with the first soft brush of his mouth against hers and intensified until her entire being was dissolving in rivers of sensation. Was flowing toward him and around him, binding her to him with invisible, inextricable strands.

He tightened his hold, sliding one hand down to cradle her bottom and anchoring the back of her head with the other. The pressure of his lips increased, testing, tasting. Her last hazy impression before her eyes fell shut was of stars spinning in the sky and the moon brazenly watching the slow-moving water ballet being enacted below. And then there was nothing but the scent of night-cooled flowers, the sweet heavy flavor of ice wine on her tongue, and a raging in her blood that defied description.

She should have put a stop to things right then. The woman she'd been up until that moment would have acknowledged there was Tommy to think of, there was the lie, the deceit. And most of all, there was Pierce and the moonlight, and she was too sophisticated not to know the consequences of allowing passion to blind her to all these other complications.

But she'd become another creature, one bewitched by kisses she had no business accepting, and consumed by a hunger that acknowledged no other protocol but its own greedy satisfaction.

When she felt his fingers skim over her shoulder, taking the strap of her swimsuit with them as they slid down her arm, she did worse than try to stop him. She helped him, angling herself in such a way that in no time at all her naked breasts sprang pale and buoyant against the muscle-sheathed planes of his chest.

She felt his gaze on her, burning a path over her flesh, and then his mouth. His tongue traced the curve of her breast and thunderheads gathered somewhere very deep within her. He found her nipple, teased it beyond endurance, and lightning arced the length of her, searing everything it touched: her heart, her soul.

She fought to contain the blood racing through her veins like fire. Opened her mouth to draw air into her beleaguered lungs, and uttered a strangled moan instead.

"Nicole," he whispered, beseeching her, and then again, more raggedly, "Nicole…?"

She knew what he was asking. Knew, too, that in allowing her head to drop back and expose the vulnerable length of her throat, she was offering herself without reservation. Without any sense of self-preservation.

The water swirled around them, warm, conspiratorial, its gentle current a seduction in itself that swept them even farther past the point of caring that what they were doing would, in time, exact a terrible price. Her legs floated up to secure themselves around his waist. She heard the low rumble in his throat, felt through the thin layers of fabric still separating them the strong, hard surge of his flesh against hers.

She was not aware that they had drifted the length of the pool until he released her long enough to hook one arm around the diving ladder suspended beside them. At that she cried out, desolated by the distance widening between them.

"I'm here," he murmured against her mouth, pulling him to her again, his legs tangling with hers.

And he was. Her swimsuit slipped to her waist, to her ankles, and with a quick flick of her feet, joined his trunks somewhere in the glimmering depths below. He was beside her, around her, and then, swiftly, smoothly, he was within her.

The lightning arced again, torching them both. Flickered and leapt in pulsing rhythm, a torment too acute to withstand. She opened her eyes, silently begging him for the release he would not grant. Black and gleaming, his hair lay flat against his skull. Water trickled down his face, spiked his eyelashes.

"Pierce," she pleaded.

He shook his head; dipped his mouth to hers, silencing her. She felt the vigor of him, the passion, the raw masculine strength. In what was surely a moment of pure madness, she wanted to whisper "I love you" and bind herself to him through eternity.

Instead, she buried her face against him. Sank her teeth softly into the sinew of his shoulder. Swallowed the small scream of delirium that filled her throat as the storm swept closer and hung poised, choosing its own time to destroy them.

There was no deflecting it. He knew that, too, although he tried to halt its progress, bracing himself against the ladder and welding her hips to his with an iron grip as if, by the sheer force of his will, he could turn aside destiny.

It was no use. She disintegrated around him, a tiny pebble lost in a flood of heat so intense that nothing of her was left except the ever-widening circles that marked her passing.

Her body still sweetly linked with his, she sagged against him, the tremors of fulfillment to which he'd brought her still echoing within. At length the din subsided and she became aware again of the soft sounds of the external world around her. The lapping of the water against the tiled wall of the pool, the sleepy chirp of a bird, the faint rustle of the breeze in the leaves of the dogwood tree.

She ventured a glance at Pierce. His head lay flung back against the top rung of the ladder. His eyes were closed. Had it not been for the vein throbbing viciously in his neck, he could have been sleeping. Yet what sort of dream carved his mouth so severely and drew his brows together in such uncompromising censure?

Despite the warmth of the night Nicole shivered, the pleasure he had brought to her swamped by the ever-present guilt lurking in the shadows. From the moment she'd met him, she'd been deceiving this man. No use now trying to mitigate her latest transgression by painting it as anything other than what it was: the greatest lie of all.

She had not made love with Pierce. Making love implied a mutual affection and trust between two people. It demanded honesty and respect. She could not offer the first, and did not deserve the second. But because she was hungry for him, she'd settled for unprotected sex and no matter how she wished she could define it otherwise, it refused to present itself in a more forgiving light.

Pierce appeared to agree with her. Even as she prepared to slip free of him, he opened his eyes and looked not *at* her but *through* her. In all her years of nursing she had never met a more empty, hopeless gaze.

And then he drew his hand down his face, as if in doing so he could wipe away everything that had transpired between the pair of them in the last half hour, and said very quietly, "Oh, damn!"

A fist seemed to close around her heart. Blindly, before the sob rising in her throat could betray her, she pushed away from him and swam underwater to the shallow end of the pool. Reaching up, she grabbed the nearest towel and shielded herself with it as she climbed the steps.

She did not know he'd followed her until her swimsuit landed with a plop at her feet. She ignored it and, tying the towel around herself sarong style, fled up the garden to the house. She could not face him again that night.

She was too afraid of what she might read in his expression.

Whatever her doubts about Pierce's feelings, however, she entertained none about Tommy's when he met the puppy. The moment he set eyes on her, his face lit up with a glow that went a long way toward easing Nicole's heartache. Dropping to his knees, he let out a squeal of undiluted joy.

For her part, Honey-Peaches raced out from under the table where she'd been busily chewing on an old tea towel knotted in the middle, and flung herself at Tommy in unabandoned ecstasy.

"I swear a body would think they were litter mates," Janet said, watching the mutual exchange with a smile. "I haven't seen that child look so happy since dear knows when. Even that benighted dog is smiling and as for her tail—it'll wag right off at the rate it's going!"

She was right. In the blur of movement of boy and dog rolling around on the floor together, Honey-Peaches wore a grin that stretched from one floppy ear to the other and quite how she remained earthbound was a mystery.

"Whether Pierce approves or not, bringing her home was the best thing I could have done," Nicole said.

"Nicole," Janet began, her voice sounding a note of caution.

"I mean it, Janet. I really don't care what our high and mighty Commander thinks and I'm quite prepared to tell him so to his face. In fact, I've had quite enough of him being the one to call all the shots around here."

"Is that so?" Pierce said from the doorway, and Nicole felt the bottom fall out of her stomach. "Then perhaps we'd better adjourn to the library where you can give free rein to your dissatisfactions without fear of corrupting innocent ears."

"We haven't had breakfast yet," she said, ticked off beyond measure at the quaver in her voice that she couldn't quite repress. He stood very tall and erect, every inch the officer not about to countenance mutiny from the ranks. A daunting figure, indeed, and about as far removed from last night's lover as was an attack-trained Doberman pinscher from a spaniel.

"Nor ever likely to at this rate," he replied, reaching down to separate squirming pup from wriggling child. "Allow me to expedite matters by keeping an eye on the mutt while you attend to your duties."

As if she knew her fate hung in the balance, Honey-Peaches switched her attentions to Pierce and proceeded to bestow affection on him with almost as much enthusiasm as she'd lavished it on Tommy. Dignity remaining intact regardless, Pierce pinned Nicole in an enigmatic stare. "I'll be in the library, Nicole. Don't keep me waiting too long."

"Well," Janet breathed, as the door swung shut behind him, "if that isn't enough to put a person off her feed! But I did try to warn you, Nicole."

"I know." Nicole blew out a sigh. "I just hope he doesn't take his annoyance out on..." She rolled her eyes to where Tommy had settled down with his bowl of cereal. "I hate to think how disappointed he'll be if the dog has to go."

"Pierce isn't that kind of man," Janet said. "Whatever his failings, he's not the kind to be unfair."

In her heart, Nicole agreed, but her belief was put to the test when she approached the library. The French doors were open and Pierce stood on the patio, brows drawn together in a frown, watching Honey-Peaches who had both paws as well as her nose planted in a bowl of milk.

Running the tip of her tongue over lips as dry as sand, Nicole murmured a faint "Ahem!" to alert him to her presence.

He looked a little startled. "I didn't hear you come in," he said, affording her the briefest glance of acknowledgment before fixing his attention on the puppy again. "I was miles away."

Considering how best to dispose of a nanny who had overstepped her place in one way too many, perhaps? Prepared for the worst, Nicole compressed her lips.

He noticed. "I've been thinking about the dog," he said, after a pause.

"You mean Honey-Peaches?" *Oh, for pity's sake, Nicole, do you see any other dog in the vicinity?*

"Exactly. Honey-Peaches will have to go. There are some things I refuse to live with."

"How can you be so callous?" Disappointment, so bitter on her tongue she could almost taste it, had her spitting the question at him.

"I beg your pardon?"

His tone and her own common sense told her to stop then, before she made a bad situation even worse, but what the heck! She'd threatened to speak her mind and she'd gone too far to back down now. "You saw Tommy's face when he was playing with the dog, the light in his eyes. How can you crush a child's happiness so unfeelingly? Or is this just your way of letting me know that, your momentary lapse of judgment last night notwithstanding, you're still the Commander, in charge of all decision making? Would you really sacrifice a helpless puppy, not to mention Tommy's well-being, just to reestablish your position of authority in this household?"

He regarded her in silence for a moment which threatened to tick into eternity. Finally, he said mildly, "I'm afraid your anxiety to paint me as the villain of the piece has led you to the wrong conclusion, Nicole. I'm not proposing to get rid of the dog, I merely object to her name. I feel like a bloody fool calling her Honey-Peaches, so you're going to have to choose between one and the other. If it matters at all, I'd prefer Peaches."

Humiliation washed over her then, wave after devastating wave. "Oh," she croaked. "I see. I...um apologize."

"There's no reason at all," he went on, appearing to be fascinated by a tub of Martha Washington pelargoniums at the edge of the patio, "why we shouldn't keep her. She seems to have a good temperament."

That he should choose now to be the soul of reason! "Thank you. I can't tell you what this will mean to Tommy. He'll be thrilled."

"Yes." Pierce switched his attention to her for a moment then swung back to the pelargoniums. "It's another very fine day," he said woodenly.

"Yes."

"Do you and Tom have any special plans?"

"No," she said, grateful that he couldn't see how her gaze roamed over him, stripping away the gray and white striped shirt and tailored charcoal slacks and recalling the body underneath. Remembering the powerful shoulders, the long, strong legs and how her hips had nested so perfectly against his. How he had held her close to him as if she were, for a brief dazzling time, the most precious thing in the world to him.

"It might be a good idea to keep him fairly quiet. He threw up on the way home last night."

Last night. Strung with tension, the words hovered reproachfully in the air. He felt it, too. "Speaking of last night," he began.

"Probably too much excitement," she said at the same time, and could have died on the spot.

To her surprise he laughed, a harshly grating sound that contained not a shred of amusement, and swung 'round to face her. "I didn't ask you in here to talk about the weather, Nicole, and I frankly don't give a damn what you call the dog. I think we both know that."

Determined to keep her mouth shut until she could be sure that what came out was something she could live with, Nicole pressed her lips together and stared at a spot next to the peony blossoms in the hearth.

"We need to talk about last night," he said, and when she gave a little moan of distress and averted her eyes, went on, "No, don't turn away from me. I feel enough of a heel as it is. Of all the mistakes I've made in my life, what I instigated last night ranks as the most unforgivable."

Stretching out one hand, he cupped her jaw and tilted it so that short of closing her eyes, she had no choice but to meet his gaze. He was such a decent man, so utterly beautiful and honorable, that it broke her heart to look at him and know how deeply he regretted what had been, for her, an unforgettable experience.

"It will not happen again," he said.

They were the same words he'd used the first time he'd kissed her but this time she couldn't drum up the fiery hauteur with which she'd repelled him then. This time she wanted to weep because much though she wished it otherwise, the simple truth was that she could not bring herself to regret what they'd shared last night. Right or wrong, it blazed in her memory, something to be hoarded and treasured against the time when he would look at her with disgust for the deception she had practiced on him.

"I hope," he said, "that you won't let...it...induce you to resign."

It. Not "lovemaking," not even "good sex." Just *it.*

"No," she said.

"Good," he said, then, just to make sure she didn't misinterpret that remark to mean he'd actually enjoyed *it,* added, "Tommy would find losing you very hard."

"I'd find it hard, too. I'm deeply fond of him." *Not to mention his guardian.*

"So we'll just..." He spread his hands helplessly, clearly at a loss for the right words.

"Forget *it* ever happened," she said bitterly, unable to suppress the hurt that persisted in ravaging her. What had she expected? That he'd feel obligated to marry her because, in a moment of inexplicable weakness, they'd succumbed to unpremeditated sex?

"I doubt I'll be able to do that," he said.

But he seemed to manage it. Over the course of the next three days, Nicole hardly saw him and he spent no time at all with Tommy. Instead of coming home for dinner, he phoned just before seven. "Say good night to Tom for me, will you? I'm working late at the office again."

Family breakfasts received the same short shrift. When she brought Tommy downstairs, Pierce was already gone for the day. That he was avoiding Nicole was clear enough, but what hurt her more was that his neglect brought about a resurgence of the insecurity Tommy had experienced in the early days after his parents' death.

"Nicole, is Uncle Pierce living with Mommy and Daddy?" he asked on the Wednesday. "Is that why he doesn't come home anymore?"

She hardly knew how to answer him.

If Pierce made himself scarce, however, Louise Trent was much in evidence, scurrying around the house, notepad and pen in hand. When she discovered Peaches had taken up residence, she wasted no time airing her opinion on the matter.

"What is this thing doing in here?" she inquired, sweeping uninvited into the kitchen just before noon on the Tuesday.

Janet, who was making bread at one end of the counter, gave her a stony stare. "If you're referring to the dog, she lives here."

"Inside the house? I can't believe Commander Warner is aware of that."

"He knows," Janet replied, pounding the bread dough savagely, and addressed her next remark to Nicole who sat at the table helping Tommy shape his own ball of dough into grimy little rolls. "You got those things ready for the oven yet?"

"Just about," Nicole said, wiping Tommy's floury hands with a damp cloth.

"I'm allergic to dogs, you know," Louise said, dabbing at her perfect nose with a scrap of lace-trimmed linen and shooing away an ecstatic Peaches who seemed unable to believe that not all people fell in love with her on sight.

"Can't say I do," Janet replied, unmoved. "Can't say I particularly care, either. The dog's here to stay."

Louise bristled. "We'll see about that. In any event, I don't want it underfoot this weekend."

"What's happening this weekend?" Nicole asked Janet, when they were alone again.

"Miss Louise has planned a housewarming party for Saturday, and guess whose house she'll be warming?" Janet sniffed scornfully. "I daresay she sees it as a dress rehearsal for when she assumes the role full time, but if she thinks she's taking over my kitchen, she can think again. Until I hear differently, I take orders from the Commander and no one else."

Nicole could think of few things she'd like less than being forced to watch Louise hanging on Pierce's arm and calling him "sweets" every second sentence. "It might be best if I take Tommy out for the day. Ms. Trent doesn't like little boys any better than she likes puppies."

"You're right," Janet said. "If it were up to her, she'd probably keep them both in a kennel at the bottom of the garden, as far away from the house as possible."

But when Nicole mentioned the idea to Pierce, managing to waylay him when he came home unexpectedly midmorning on the Thursday to pick up something he needed at the office, he was adamant. "Absolutely not. I want Tom here."

"Why?" she said. "He won't enjoy being passed around among strangers, especially not at that time of day. He's past his best by six."

"He can put in an early appearance and still be in bed

by seven." He shuffled through the papers on his desk, then swiped them aside in a rare show of temper. "Have you let him play in here when I wasn't around? I can't find a damn thing in this mess."

"No, I have not let him play in here when you weren't around," she snapped back, outraged as much by the way he absolutely refused to look her in the eye as by his unjust accusation. "Not, of course, that he hasn't had ample opportunity, since you're so seldom around here lately. I'd be surprised if he even recognizes you the next time you deign to put in an appearance."

"I am still on the Navy payroll, Nicole, and I do happen to have a job to do," Pierce informed her, the steel in his voice reflected in his eyes as he spared her a fleeting glare. "A very demanding job, in case you're interested. And you should be since it's what enables me to afford this house. And you."

It was the *And you* that pushed her over the edge, as if, on top of everything else he had to put up with, he was saddled with paying off a woman he'd used. "I'll be happy to take a cut in salary, if it will ease your burden, Commander, and I can assure you Tommy would be happy to settle for a less opulent lifestyle if it meant he could enjoy more quality time with the man who's supposed to be standing in for his father."

"Oh, for Christ's sake, don't you think I know that?" He slammed a heavy manual down on the desk so hard, the aftershock sent a sheaf of papers fluttering to the ground. "I can only do so much and just lately it seems as if everything's getting away from me. I have specs to present for a new destroyer, meetings to attend, business trips I should be making and which keep getting put off because personal matters keep getting in the way. And on top of all that, I'm supposed to whip this library into shape so that people can traipse through here on the weekend and tell me what a nice, tight ship I run."

"You've also got a child and he comes before any of

that. Get your priorities straight, for heaven's sake! Other men manage to.''

He sent her another scorching glare. "Well, I'm not other men. This isn't the future I had mapped out for myself, in case you aren't aware. Being invalided out of active service was bad enough, but trying to juggle a new career *and* having instant fatherhood foisted on me before I'd had time to catch my breath—well, let me tell you, it's taking some getting used to!''

"And you've still got a long way to go," she replied bitingly. "Or do you think you're the only one suffering here? What about Tommy? To hell with your shattered dreams—what about his?''

Her words hit home. He stopped his frantic searching and dragged a weary hand over his face. "You're right and I'm sorry if you feel I'm letting Tom down. Believe me, that's the last thing I want. Whatever else you think about me, Nicole, rest assured that, prepared or not, I'm certainly willing to shoulder full responsibility for him. Ungrudgingly. I'm not so small-minded that I can't love another man's child, and most especially not Jim's child. Tom's as much a part of my life and of what goes on in this house as anyone, which is why I want him here on Saturday night, even if it is only for a few minutes.''

"Fine. I'll have him dressed and ready to go on display by six, and collect him again about seven," she said, and turned to go.

His next words stopped her in her tracks. "I want you there, too.''

"I can't imagine why," she said, swinging back to face him. "Employees aren't usually included in social events.''

He heaved a sigh, as though what he had to say next was costing him more than he cared to think about. "You're something more than an employee, Nicole.''

Indeed she was, but not in the way he understood. It was hard enough maintaining the lies with him, without having to do so to all his friends, as well. "I'd prefer not to—"

"I won't take no for an answer."

"Is that an order, Commander?" she asked, resenting the way he used his authority to coerce her when it suited him.

His lips tightened in displeasure as much, she suspected, at her tone as the question itself. "If that's what it takes, yes, it's an order." He paused as if he expected her to salute, then back submissively out of the room.

She did neither. Instead, she returned his gaze, her own sparking with indignation. "As you wish, Commander."

Anger flushed under his skin at that, highlighting his cheekbones and flinging his eyes into electric blue relief. "I wish," he snapped, all towering senior officer addressing an insubordinate junior. "You are, after all, being paid to put in a full working day."

"And what about the evenings?" she flung back, the sheer cruelty of his reminder blinding her to everything but the urge to hurt him as deeply as he'd just wounded her. "Or do you expect to have those thrown in free as a form of entertainment when nothing better presents itself?"

The blood drained from his face abruptly, leaving him blanched with shock. "If that's your opinion of the kind of man I am," he said hoarsely, "then I can't imagine why you're still here at all and I will certainly understand if you wish to resign."

Too late she regretted the self-indulgence of lashing out at him. Pierce wasn't the only one who needed to rearrange his priorities; her own were getting sadly out of whack, too. "I'm here," she replied, gathering the rags of her dignity around her, "because Tommy needs me and I will not abandon him because you and I—"

"Exactly," he said. "Tommy needs you. You make him feel secure and safe. If he misbehaves or is feeling out of sorts, no one handles him better than you do. And that's all I meant when I asked you to be here with him on Saturday evening.''

She had no business feeling let down by his reply. What else had she expected him to say? That because she'd let him make love to her, he'd feel obligated to treat her as an equal? As someone who mattered to him in any capacity other than that of Tommy's nanny? That he'd seek her out for the sheer pleasure of her company?

From somewhere beyond the hurt, she drummed up a shrug of indifference. ''I understand perfectly. And now, if you'll excuse me, I'll get back to earning my salary.''

She got as far as the door before he stopped her, his voice once again tight with anger. ''Don't do this, Nicole.''

She remained with her hand on the knob and her back toward him. ''What is it I'm doing that displeases you?''

''Playing the woman scorned. Adopting an adversarial attitude to a relationship that—''

''We don't have a relationship, Commander,'' she flared, spinning 'round to face him again. ''We have, as you so succinctly reminded me less than five minutes ago, a contract.''

He subjected her to a long, level scrutiny, his blue eyes unreadable. She stared back, manufacturing all the hurt that insisted on welling up and swamping her, into icy rage. It was her only defense against him. If she allowed herself to remember the tenderness, the passion.... Oh, sweet heaven, if she remembered all that, she'd dissolve in tears and subject herself to further humiliation.

He held her gaze interminably, then finally lifted his shoulders in a shrug situated somewhere between frustration and resignation. ''I see. I'm sorry you feel that way. I was hoping we could be friends.''

If he'd offered her friendship the day she met him, she'd have been happy to accept. Friendship would have precluded the need for lies and left the door open for love to grow. But the complications inherent in her deceit precluded such a simple outcome and there was no going back. There'd been no going back from the moment she'd presented herself as someone other than who she really was.

The best she could hope for was that, when he learned the truth about her, he'd understand her motives and forgive her. Perhaps then they could be friends. The fact that it would no longer be enough to satisfy her was a disappointment she'd have to bear alone.

Breakfast was scarcely finished on Saturday morning when the show began. Vans rolled up the driveway and Louise's minions poured into the house. Florists vied with caterers for kitchen counter space; musicians tangled with electricians in the library.

"In my day, a housewarming party meant a few friends dropping by with a plant," Janet muttered, watching events from the deck outside the kitchen where she and Nicole, with Tommy and Peaches, had sought escape from the crowd. "I can't believe the Commander wanted this kind of shindig."

But it struck Nicole that Pierce seemed more than willing to give Louise a free hand. Shortly after the hubbub began, he once again made an excuse about having to attend to business in his downtown office and vacated the premises. No one saw him again until late afternoon.

By then, Louise had orchestrated a transformation. Gorgeous arrangements of flowers adorned the reception rooms. Linen-covered tables dotted the patio around the pool. Colored lights threaded the trees and shrubs. A pianist coaxed Broadway selections from the concert grand in the living room. A string quartet played Mozart on the terrace outside the library. A fleet of uniformed maids and waiters stood ready to serve chilled Veuve Clicquot and the trays of elegant hors d'oeuvres created by the army of caterers.

Crystal sparkled, silver dazzled, furniture gleamed. But nothing quite outshone the hostess. Louise was a vision in emerald taffeta complemented with teardrop diamond earrings and the subtle aura of Gio by Armani.

"If that hemline of hers was any shorter," Janet declared, perching on the side of Tommy's bathtub as Nicole readied him for the party, "it'd meet her plunging neckline. That's one woman who doesn't believe in leaving a lot to a man's imagination."

"Well, you can hardly blame her for wanting to look her best. She's gone to a lot of trouble to make the evening a success," Nicole said, trying to be fair.

"And she's had a good time doing it, too. This whole affair promises to be the most extravagant outlay of that hussy's energy and the Commander's money since the day she first hooked her claws into him and talked him into buying this house."

"You're very fond of Pierce, aren't you?" Nicole said, trying unsuccessfully to tame Tommy's cowlick. They were due to present themselves downstairs in another fifteen minutes and she was having a hard time convincing him he had to look his best.

"Why wouldn't I be? I've known him since he was a boy. Looked after his folks' house until they retired to Arizona, and was first in line when he needed someone to run this place. Not that I expect to be kept on when milady moves in. I'm not fancy enough for her." She ran a critical eye over Nicole's plain blue blouse and skirt. "Speaking of fancy, I hope that's not what you're planning to wear downstairs."

"What's wrong with it?"

"It looks like a uniform. The only things missing are the white shoes and stockings."

Although she and Janet had grown quite close with the passing weeks and often chatted over morning coffee or in the afternoon while Tommy napped, their conversations seldom ventured into personal areas, so Nicole was somewhat taken aback by such frank disapproval. "Well," she said lightly, "I can produce them, too, if you think they'll improve matters."

Janet tipped her head to one side and fixed Nicole in a very old-fashioned look. "Who are you trying to fool, Nicole?"

The fear of having her deceit exposed had grown no less for all that she'd succeeded in concealing it so well all these weeks. Janet's question brought it right to the forefront again and sent Nicole's pulse into spasms of flickering anxiety. "What do you mean?"

Janet pursed her lips. "I might be past sixty but that doesn't mean I can't see what's going on under my nose."

Nicole's heart stopped dead at that. "I really don't know what you're talking about," she insisted, dry-mouthed.

"You're a pretty woman, Nicole. You're too smart not to know it and so is the Commander. I see him watching you, the same way I see you sneaking looks his way when you think he's not noticing."

"Oh, nonsense!"

"Furthermore," Janet continued, unperturbed, "there's a softness to you, a womanliness if you like, that Louise Trent will never have no matter how hard she tries to mold herself to fit the part."

"She's a very successful businesswoman. She hardly needs to worry about fitting any other role."

"She's too aggressive. Oh, she might know how to close a real estate deal and there's no one better when it comes to putting on the sales pressure, but you're the kind of woman a man like Pierce Warner marries. So why do you go to such lengths to make yourself look as plain as possible? Why are you afraid to show yourself off in your best light?"

"I'm just a paid employee, Janet."

"Hogwash! That's the sort of rubbish women my age might believe but you modern things know better. Leave Tommy with me and go put on something eye-catching. Give that Trent creature a run for her money, instead of leaving her a clear field."

"No," Nicole said. "I don't think Pierce would appreciate my seeming to push my way into a social occasion that clearly doesn't include me."

"He won't appreciate your showing up looking as if he pays you so poorly that you can't spring for something a bit fancier than a plain old cotton skirt and blouse, either."

"I don't have anything—"

"Save your breath. I do the laundry around here, remember, and I've seen the inside of your closet. You've got plenty of pretty things to wear." Janet hauled Tommy onto her lap and jerked her head in the direction of Nicole's suite. "Go on. Show the Commander what he's been missing all this time."

Was it vanity that made the idea irresistible, or simply that the real Nicole Bennett had been locked away for so long that she couldn't withstand the chance to be free for a while? Whatever the reason, Nicole found herself back in her suite and riffling through the dresses hanging in her closet.

Careful, a little voice reminded her. *This could backfire. Appear too sophisticated and you'll arouse suspicion. You don't need anyone asking awkward questions. Forget the designer silk, the Italian dinner dress, the sequins and the beads. They shriek money you're not supposed to have.*

Heeding the advice, she chose a plain cream sundress cinched at the waist with a broad satin belt. Her grandmother's sapphire earrings would have added a nice touch of contrast, but it seemed safer to rely for decoration on the tan she'd acquired and the plain string of pearls which had been her parents' graduation gift.

"Lovely," Janet said, appearing uninvited at her door with Tommy in tow. "I've always liked it when you do up your hair on top of your head like that, with those bits of curls hanging loose."

Nicole took a last look in the mirror. "You think I'll do?"

"You'll stop traffic," Janet assured her.

She didn't quite do that, but she did put a dent in the buzz of conversation when she came downstairs with Tommy clinging to her hand. People wandering through the front hall turned to watch as she threaded her way among them and went in search of Pierce. Some of them smiled, a few greeted her but most commented to each other.

"That's the child..."

"Pierce was named legal guardian...the nearest living relative, you know..."

Not quite, Nicole thought.

"She must be the nanny. I heard he'd hired one..."

"...no one knows much about her...new to town, I understand. Came from down east somewhere..."

"Young, isn't she?"

"Young and beautiful... I expected a much older woman..."

Once upon a time, Nicole would have moved easily in such a gathering. Her parents were wealthy; they entertained often and well. From her mother she had learned to compile an elegant menu, from her father to know the difference between a wine that was merely excellent and one that was magnificent. But tonight she felt like Cinderella, afraid that her disguise would slip and reveal her for the impostor she was.

The guests' curiosity, though not unkindly meant, burned holes in her and made her wish she'd stuck to her original outfit of the serviceable blouse and skirt. She didn't want to stand out in the crowd or be the focus of interest; she wanted to fade quietly into the background, a nondescript accessory unworthy of notice.

"I was beginning to think you were going to stand me up." Suddenly Pierce was looming in front of her, blocking her path.

She saw him inspecting her, saw the approval in his eyes as they took note of her hair, the pearls at her throat, the low-cut square neckline of her dress which revealed

only the merest hint of cleavage but which, under his
scrutiny, struck her as gapingly indecent.

"Here's Tommy," she said, thrusting the child at his
uncle and preparing to bolt back the way she'd come.
"I'll leave you to introduce him to everybody."

"Not so fast." He caught her elbow and guided her
toward the library where most of the guests seemed to
have congregated. "You're part of the package, remember? I want people to meet you, too."

"I'd really much rather—"

"How about a drink?" He collared a waiter and
pressed a glass of champagne in her hand.

"No, really, Pierce, I'd just as soon not. I'm here in
a working capacity."

"Consider yourself off-duty then." He placed the flat
of his hand against her back, just above the top of her
dress, and urged her forward. His flesh lay warm against
hers, an unnerving reminder of how it had felt when he'd
touched her intimately that other time.

Involuntarily, she shrank from the contact.

"Relax, Nicole," he murmured. "We're surrounded
by people. Your virtue's safe."

More's the pity! she thought. "It never occurred to
me to think otherwise," she said, holding her head high
and stalking through the claustrophobic confines of the
library to the garden.

Quite a crowd had gathered there already, clustered in
sociable groups on the lawns and patios. When Pierce
appeared with Tommy, the guests converged on him, full
of sympathetic cluckings like so many old hens.

"Most of you know Tom," he said, drawing Nicole
forward when she tried to shrink into the background,
"but I don't think you've met the woman who's re-
sponsible for putting the smile back on his face. This is
his nanny, Nicole Bennett."

They nodded and smiled, shook her hand and wel-
comed her; told her what a fine job she was doing and
how lucky Pierce was to have found her. She smiled

back and endured their kindness the best way she knew how, all too aware that Louise recognized her whipped cream sundress for the expensive garment it was. She eyed Nicole with the same suspicion she'd have regarded a black widow spider.

Ignoring her, Nicole watched as Tommy dealt with his first cocktail party. Small wonder the women melted at the sight of him. He looked adorable in his navy shorts and red and white striped shirt. His hair had bleached in the sun, making his blue eyes even more beautiful, and his skin shone with health and cleanliness.

She saw him smile, heard him say "Hi," in his sweet little boy's voice, watched him cling to Pierce's hand when well-meaning strangers tried to hug him, and felt her heart overflow with love.

He was, she decided, worth every last lie she'd had to tell. She'd tell them all again in a heartbeat if it meant her being able to be near him like this.

She had no idea someone was studying her just as closely until a vaguely familiar voice said quietly, "Your obvious affection for Arlene's son is quite remarkable. If one didn't know better, one might almost think you were related to him."

Shocked, she spun around and found herself face to face with the woman she'd met in the restaurant, the day she'd spent the afternoon at the market in the park. The woman who'd been Arlene's best friend.

"My goodness!" she stammered, the panic that was never far from the surface rising up to confound her further. "It's you!"

"Indeed it is, and the name's Alice Holt," Arlene's friend replied. "May I say I find it a quite amazing coincidence that we should meet again here, of all places, in the home where my late friend's son is now living? I think we should talk about that, don't you?"

Before she could answer, Nicole sensed herself being watched from another source. Glancing up, she saw Louise standing in the open doorway of the library, her beautiful hazel eyes blazing with anger and suspicion. Waving aside a waiter who stopped to speak to her, she stepped out onto the patio and strode purposefully forward.

So this was how it was going to end, Nicole thought, closing her eyes. With her cornered and exposed as a liar in front of half the population of Morningside. So much for the lies having been worth it. After this, she'd be lucky if she spent another night under the same roof with Tommy, let alone be allowed to look after him.

CHAPTER SIX

"I DON'T believe Commander Pierce expects you to engage his guests in conversation, Miss Bennett," Louise said coldly, assessing Nicole's pearls. "I rather think he'd prefer it if you were to wait in the nursery until he's ready to send for you."

"You're mistaken on two counts, Louise," Arlene's friend interrupted. "I'm the one who engaged Miss Bennett in conversation and I don't think Pierce minds at all. Here he comes now, in fact, so why don't we ask him?"

"That's not necessary," Louise began, but Arlene's friend wasn't easily stopped once she'd engaged gears.

"Pierce," she called out, "I'm having a lovely chat with Miss Bennett. You don't mind, do you?"

"Why would I?" His smile was charmingly relaxed. "Keep her down here as long as you can, Alice. She won't believe me when I tell her she's a welcome addition to the party, but she might listen to you."

"But what about Tommy?" Desperate to escape, Nicole scanned the garden, looking for him. "I don't see him anywhere."

"He was heading for the house, the last I saw of him," Pierce said. "Said something about checking up on Peaches."

"Dear God! First the nanny, now the dog! What's next, I wonder?" Louise muttered, *sotto voce*.

Distracted by a couple of late arrivals, Pierce appeared not to have heard. "Who invited the Mayor, for Pete's sake?"

"I did, of course." All smiles in less time than it took to blink, Louise slipped her arm through Pierce's and

drew him toward the newcomers. "He's a powerful man
to have in your corner, sweetie, should you ever need
one, and I happen to know he's also in the market for a
new house."

"And a good thing he showed up when he did," Alice
remarked dryly. "Our esteemed hostess was about to
lose it at the thought of being upstaged by a dog."

As if to give credence to Louise's misgivings, however, Peaches came skidding out of the library just then.
Delighted at being freed from confinement in the laundry
room, the puppy charged madly across the lawn, weaving an erratic path between guests with Tommy in gleeful pursuit. Tables wobbled precariously, one of the
maids serving canapes almost ended up wearing them,
and there were subdued shrieks from more than one
quarter at the trail of spattered champagne left in the
duo's wake.

"Please excuse me," Nicole said to Alice. "I think
I'd better take charge of this before things get really out
of hand."

"By all means." Alice's eyes were full of specula-
tion—or was it certainty? "But we must talk later, my
dear, when things have settled down."

"Yes." Nicole said, afraid Arlene's friend had
jumped to some all-too-accurate conclusions and knowing, if that were so, that she must be persuaded to keep
them to herself, at least for the time being. "I think we
must. Tommy goes to bed at seven and I'll be in my
suite as soon as he's settled for the night. It's the third
door to the left at the top of the stairs, right next to the
nursery."

"Excellent. At least there we'll be assured of privacy
and can talk without fear of being overheard.
Meanwhile..." With an amused nod, Alice indicated the
flurry of commotion taking place on the lawn. "...some-
where in that crowd there's a small boy and a dog bent
on creating mayhem, so don't let me keep you."

Grateful for the reprieve, no matter how temporary,

Nicole set out to corral her charges. She finally ran Peaches to earth on the deck outside the kitchen. Pierce had a firm grip on her collar, but of her nephew there was no sign.

"I'm sorry about this," Nicole panted. "I should have kept a closer eye on Tommy. We'd made sure the dog was shut in the laundry room before the party began and it just never occurred to me he'd decide to let her out like that."

Pierce squatted down to fondle the puppy's ears. "No real harm's been done. I've agreed she can stay out as long as she's not running wild and upsetting people. Tom's inside now, looking for her leash."

Nicole could only imagine how Louise would react to that news. "Miss Trent is right, you know, Pierce. This is a very elegant affair, and I'm not sure having a puppy on the scene is appropriate."

"I'm not a hundred per cent certain myself," he admitted, "but Tom persuaded me otherwise." He looked up, his blue eyes alight with wry amusement. "When I suggested putting her back in the laundry room, he flung himself down on the deck here and threw a tantrum. Frankly, I'd have agreed to let her dance in the middle of the buffet table if that's what it had taken to shut him up."

"I was afraid something like that might happen," Nicole said, trying to ignore the way his gaze fused with hers, alive with unspoken reminders of the last time she'd been alone with him in the night and nothing but the rising moon to witness the exchange. "This sort of event at the end of a long, hot day is a bit more than a four-year-old can handle with equanimity."

"And what about you, Nicole?" Pierce asked softly. "How's your equanimity holding up?"

Her knees threatened to buckle under the probing intensity of his regard. But it wasn't love that charged the air with sudden electricity, it was unadorned lust, she told herself, choosing the ugly word in the hope that it would tarnish the emotions swirling between him and her. But nothing soothed the clenching need inside her, the stabbing, involuntary spasm so well hidden from the naked eye.

"My equanimity," she said shakily, "is holding up well enough that I could have dealt with Tommy. You should have stayed with your guests and left me to look after all this. That's why I'm here after all."

"I would have, but you were deep in conversation with Alice Holt. It was easier to handle things myself." Without warning, Pierce reached up and grasped her hand. His touch sent a flush of heat shooting from her toes to her cheeks. "And just for the record, Nicole, you're here because I want you here. Can we please forget that ugly scene in the library, the other day? You've got to know that I value you far too much ever to put a dollar value on what you've brought to Tom's life—and to mine."

He sounded so sincere, it would have been easy to convince herself that he meant more than he said, that he needed her, wanted her, in a way that had nothing to do with Tommy.

The trouble was, everything came back to Tommy in ways Pierce couldn't possibly begin to guess and Nicole had the sinking feeling that the story she'd so painstakingly woven about herself was starting to unravel. Once that happened, it was a matter of time only before Pierce realized he'd been duped from the start.

How anxious would he then be for her company? How willing to believe that she hadn't deliberately set out to seduce him in order to further her own ends? If only she hadn't agreed to join him for that drink by the pool...or, failing that, if only she hadn't worn the daring swimsuit that had been an invitation to trouble all by itself.

Regret for so many things drew an involuntary sigh from her. Misreading her response in some way, Pierce pulled her closer and dropped a kiss on the back of her hand, a brief, impulsive tenderness that moved her inexpressibly. "You look lovely tonight, Nicole. I've wanted to tell you that from the minute you came downstairs."

Behind him and a little to his right, where the vine-covered pergola curved around the side of the house away from the kitchen, a movement caught Nicole's attention. Louise stood watching their exchange, her emerald taffeta dress well camouflaged by the leaves. Her expression gave away nothing of what she was feeling but her hands were clenched into fists at her sides.

"You belong with your guests, Pierce," Nicole said, hurriedly withdrawing her hand. "Leave Peaches with me and go back to your party."

She knew, from the way his brows drew together in a frown, that he was about to argue the point but she didn't give him the chance. Seizing the puppy, she fled into the kitchen. It was twenty minutes to seven already. In less than an hour she'd be facing Alice Holt. She didn't need a second confrontation with Louise. One showdown a day was enough.

Straightening up, Pierce massaged the small of his back where the old spinal injury still caught him unawares at times, and wondered what he'd said or done to send her scurrying off like that.

Hell, at times like this, he missed the Navy. Not because he was all that fond of war but because, compared to civilian life, service at sea was uncomplicated. Rules were laid down and adhered to, expectations were clear. There were no hidden meanings, no ambiguities, no subtle signals. Communication was straightforward and aboveboard. He understood men and how their minds worked.

Women, on the other hand, baffled him.

He wasn't a stupid man. He'd had his share of women and knew they found him attractive enough. Yet he never quite connected with them at some level and it had always been with a certain sense of relief that he'd returned from furlough to a life virtually free of feminine interference. Love, romantic love at least, had been a non-issue, something to be dealt with at a more convenient time.

When he'd suddenly found himself standing in as father to a four-year-old, he'd thought, fool that he was, that by hiring a nanny, he'd be making life easier for everyone. But from the minute she'd set foot in the house, Nicole had brought him nothing but complications.

He didn't understand her, he didn't know how to deal with her. She turned his orderly life upside-down and usurped his authority every chance she could. Yet despite all that, the damnable fact remained: he enjoyed every minute of aggravation she brought to his life.

He found himself watching her—*spying* on her, for crying out loud!—as she interacted with Tom. He was blown away by her patience and tenderness with the boy. He'd even gone so far as to wonder how she'd be with a child of her own, with a baby. *His* baby. The image that had swum into his mind at that held a fascination he couldn't dismiss. And that was about as contrary to what he'd expected, the day he'd hired her, as it was possible to get.

He'd wrestled with the problem for days, afraid to trust his feelings. Was it love he felt for her—or need? After all, he'd gone thirty-five years without contemplating marriage. Was it likely he'd decide in favor of it in the space of a month or two, or had his feelings more to do with convenience?

No, more than that was involved and he might as well face up to the fact. Whatever else his shortcomings, he prided himself on preserving his integrity. He neither understood nor tolerated deception, not in himself or other people.

''Well, for heaven's sake, I've run you to earth at last and just look at you! You're covered in dog hair.'' Louise's husky reproach floated out of the dusk, a reminder that Nicole wasn't his only complication. Sooner, rather than later, he was going to have to spell things out for Louise.

He buried a sigh. "It comes with the territory, Louise. We've got a pup living in the house now. What brings you back here? You don't normally frequent the kitchen porch."

"I just told you, I was looking for you," she said, dabbing at her nose with a tissue. "You're not being very sociable, Pierce. Our guests are wondering what they've done to drive you into hiding."

Your guests, Louise, he thought irritably. He couldn't put a name to half the faces swarming around his property.

She slipped a hand beneath his arm and gazed up at him soulfully. "Aren't you having a good time, sweets? You seem a bit out of sorts."

He curbed the temptation to tell her bluntly that he couldn't wait for the evening to end. She'd worked hard to make it a success, to show him how much of herself she was prepared to invest in a relationship with him.

A week ago he'd probably have viewed her efforts with more tolerance if not more enthusiasm, but a lot had happened in the last week. His growing fascination with Nicole had culminated in his making love to her and that had changed everything. But now was not the time to tell Louise that what he'd suspected for some time had crystallized into certainty: he saw no future for them as a couple.

"Pierce? What are you thinking?"

"That you're right," he said, hating having to dissemble. "We really should be mingling."

"You're sure there's nothing else troubling you?"

Her voice rang sharp with anxiety, as if she sensed trouble on the horizon. It was enough to convince him there was something to that women's intuition business, after all. "Nothing I care to go into now," he said, unwilling to tell her a direct lie. "We'll talk some other time."

"Is it the nanny, Pierce?"

He realized immediately that in trying to evade the issue, he'd made a serious tactical error. Although she managed to sound sympathetic rather than alarmed, the way she dug her nails into his arm betrayed an uneasy suspicion. "Why would you jump to that assumption, Louise?"

"Because I can't help noticing how ineffectual she is. Take this evening, for example. Where was she when you needed her? Schmoozing with the guests and leaving you to take over the job she's being paid to do." She stopped long enough to sneeze and dab again at her nose.

"Are you coming down with a cold?" he asked, with rather more optimism than was polite. "If you are, don't feel you have to stay here to run things."

"I don't have a cold, Pierce," she said reproachfully. "The dog's making me sneeze. I've mentioned a number of times that I'm allergic to it."

When he made no comment to that, she swayed against him and tucked her arm more securely in his. "But to get back to what we were talking about, sweets, someone needs to spell out to Miss Bennett exactly where her duties lie, and it might come more easily from another woman. Would you like me to talk to her?"

"No, thanks," he said. "I have no problem speaking plainly when the occasion calls for it."

"As you like." She sniffed delicately. "The offer stands, though, if ever you decide to take me up on it. I'm in this for the long haul, Pierce, you know that."

He was afraid he did. Severing the ties with Louise wasn't going to be easy or pretty. Peace-keeping in the Persian Gulf had been a breeze beside such bulldog tenacity.

By the time Peaches was securely leashed, it was almost seven. "Just enough time to make the rounds and say good night to everyone, then bedtime for you,'' Nicole told Tommy, immensely relieved that she'd soon have a valid excuse to leave the party. "Remember your manners, darling.''

He managed so beautifully for the first few minutes, submitting with good grace to the occasional hug from the women or handshake from the men, that Nicole just about burst with pride. Inevitably, though, they came to where Louise sat with a group of friends, and it was then that things fell apart in spectacular fashion.

Approaching, Tommy stared at Louise in mute fascination. Aware of her audience, Louise put on her best mother-in-waiting act. "Hello, dear,'' she said, sounding somewhat congested. "Have you come to say good night to Auntie Louise?''

Tommy said nothing and simply continued to observe her closely. With mounting dismay, Nicole saw what it was that had captured his attention. A small piece of Kleenex tissue had lodged itself at the corner of one of Louise's nostrils which were quite red, as if she'd been blowing her nose repeatedly and which made the scrap of white all the more noticeable.

She began to twitch under Tommy's scrutiny. "It's rude to stare, Thomas,'' she said, smiling fixedly. "Hasn't your nanny taught you that?''

Tommy's gaze remained glued to her face, his eyes wide and serious. Finally, he spoke. "You've got something hanging out of your nose,'' he said wonderingly.

It was such a classic line that Nicole couldn't help herself. A snort of laughter rose up in her throat and although she did her best to smother it, she didn't quite succeed. Others who'd heard seemed similarly afflicted. At length, the woman sitting beside Louise leaned over and whispered in her ear.

Scarlet with outrage and embarrassment, Louise brushed furiously at her nose. "Get that benighted creature away from me!'' she snapped, any pretense at being

Mother Earth quickly erased by the malevolent glare she shot at Peaches. "It's no wonder I'm so stuffed up that I can hardly breathe!"

Turning aside to hide another unforgivable smirk, Nicole met Pierce's amused gaze. "I'm afraid we've disgraced ourselves," she said.

"I'm afraid you have," he murmured, laughter rippling in his voice. "It really isn't polite to snigger at someone else's expense, Nicole. I'm shocked! Take that little rascal away before he voices a few more home truths."

"It's no laughing matter, Pierce. Miss Trent isn't going to forgive any of us for this."

"I can't say I blame her," he replied, but his smile and the way his gaze roamed over her took away any sting in his words. "Put the little devils to bed, both of them, then come back down here and let's try to effect some damage control."

"I'd prefer not to do that. This isn't my party, Pierce, and I feel out of place. Furthermore, I don't think Louise is going to accept an apology even if I felt disposed to offer one."

"In that case," he said, stroking the flat of his hand over her bare shoulder and urging her out of earshot of the others, "wait until everyone's gone, then come down. There's something I've been meaning to talk to you about and I don't think I can put it off any longer." Then, as added inducement in case she argued the point, "It has to do with Tommy's future and I'd like your feedback on what I'm proposing to do."

A quiver of alarm shot through her. "You're not thinking of sending him away to school or anything like that, are you?"

"No," he said, his hand still lingering. "I have something quite different in mind and it does involve you. So I'll expect to see you later, when we've got the house to ourselves again?"

"All right," she said, apprehension a leaden lump in

the pit of her stomach. His decidedly furtive air made her very nervous.

All the time that she was bathing Tommy and putting him to bed, her mind worried at the mystery. In fact, she was so totally wrapped up in it that she quite forgot she had another meeting planned for that evening and was startled to find Alice Holt standing beside the writing desk when she returned to her sitting room.

"I hope you don't mind that I let myself in," Alice said. "It made more sense than my hanging around in the hall where, if anyone had seen me, I might have had to explain myself."

"I don't mind," Nicole said, but she did. She minded very much that, if she'd been so inclined, Alice could have snooped through the contents of the desk drawer and found the evidence she needed to expose Nicole as a fraud. She minded enough to add sharply, "Have you found what you were looking for?"

Alice had the grace to blush slightly. "No," she said, "though I admit I was tempted. But I decided you deserved the chance to state your case first."

"Thank you for that much." Nicole sighed and dropped onto the love seat next to the window. "You've figured out who I really am, haven't you?"

"I think you're an impostor and my common sense tells me I should expose you as such. For reasons I fail to understand, you're cashing in on a slight physical resemblance to my late and very dear friend in order to get close either to her son or to Pierce Warner. The unsettling thing is, that slight physical resemblance to Arlene predisposes me to like you and that is the only excuse I can offer for not confronting you in public."

Alice sat down at the desk and very deliberately crossed one knee over the other, as though to signal her determination not to be hornswoggled a minute longer. "My conscience, however, is beginning to trouble me sorely, so I'd like it very much if you'd explain the reasons behind this elaborate charade you've as good as admitted you're playing.''

"I'm Arlene's sister.''

Alice laughed. "That's preposterous! Arlene didn't have a sister. She was an only child. Her mother couldn't have any more children after she was born and I know that for a fact.''

"Her 'mother' couldn't have children, period. Arlene was adopted when she was eighteen months old but she found that out only a few months before she died. Our birth mother gave us up because she felt unable to provide us with the sort of life she thought we deserved after our father deserted us.''

For a moment Alice simply stared, apparently struck speechless. Finally, she swallowed and said, "And you can prove that, can you?''

Nicole gestured at the desk. "It's all there, in a brown envelope at the bottom of the drawer. See for yourself.''

"No.'' Alice shook her head, as though to sort into some sort of order the questions burning to be asked. "I'd rather have you explain. Why, for instance, didn't Arlene confide in me if, as you claim, she'd known for months before her death that she had a sister?''

"We'd decided to keep it quiet until we'd had a chance to get to know each other again. I only found out myself last August, then spent most of the winter trying to trace her. Her adoptive parents, when I tracked them down, refused to help me locate her. They said they'd washed their hands of her when she married and wanted nothing further to do with her.''

"I can believe that,'' Alice said. "The Goodmans are very possessive. That was one of the reasons Arlene and Jim decided to make their home out here, away from their stifling influence.''

"Well, I was just as determined not to be put off, and my parents—my adoptive parents, that is—were wonderful. They helped me and encouraged me every step of the way. I finally found Arlene in February.''

"But you chose not to visit until after she died?" Alice looked skeptical. "That has a fishy ring to it. What kept you away until then?"

"My work, the weather in the Midwest. Late winter isn't the best time to drive across the prairies. But we wrote to each other and talked often on the phone. We'd planned our reunion for early June. We'd thought we'd spend a few days alone, just the four of us..."

Unexpectedly, the grief that recently had begun to subside rose up to choke Nicole again, and with it came the anger. "I was already on my way here when the accident happened. I was due to arrive on the first Thursday in June and she was killed the preceding Saturday. It was a vicious, cruel twist of fate that, after losing one another for all those years, we missed each other again by such a close margin, and I will never forgive God for taking her away like that."

Unable to sit still a moment longer with the rage she'd thought she'd dealt with again tearing at her, she leapt to her feet, snapped on the desk lamp, and wrenched open the bottom drawer. "Go ahead. Read what's in the damned envelope if you don't believe me."

Alice subjected her to a long, thoughtful stare before slowly withdrawing the envelope from its hiding place beneath a copy of the local telephone directory, then coming to sit next to Nicole on the love seat.

Struggling to compose herself, Nicole turned away and stared out at the scene in the garden below. The sun had dipped below the horizon and left only a pink stain on the ocean to mark its path. The remaining light had that peculiar pre-dark quality to it that threw the flowers into a subdued neon brilliance at the same time that it emphasized the dusky shadows.

The string quartet had finished performing and a few couples were dancing on the patio to the strains of the piano coming from the open windows of the living room. Fully recovered from her earlier humiliation, Louise Trent presided over a small contingent of well-heeled cronies, seemingly engaged in extolling the virtues of her real estate perspicacity if her expansive gestures toward the house itself were any indication.

Pierce stood some distance away, deep in discussion with three other men, one of whom Nicole knew was a colleague. But most people were lined up at a cloth-covered buffet table where a chef in a tall white hat was serving lobster thermidor.

To all intents and purposes, the evening was as highly successful and picture perfect as Nicole's life had been the day she'd set out to drive from Madison, Wisconsin, to Morningside, Oregon. How quickly it all could change, though. By an out of control truck crossing the centre line of a twisting coastal road, or simply by a word, the fabric of so many lives could be ripped apart and never put back together again.

Behind her, Nicole heard the rustle of papers and a quiet sigh. "My dear," Alice Holt said, her voice hushed with shock, "I'm so very sorry. What a truly dreadful time you must have had since you got here. But what I can't comprehend is why you haven't confided in Pierce. He would understand."

"If he would," Nicole said, "I had no way of knowing it, the day I arrived on his doorstep. He'd just been awarded guardianship of a child who was more closely related by blood to me than to him. How do you know he wouldn't have seen me as a threat to his custodial rights? *I* would have, had the situation been reversed. And I'd have moved heaven and earth to stop an outsider from trying to take Tommy away from me."

"Is that what you wanted, to take Tommy away from him? Is that what this is all about, Nicole?"

"No," Nicole said miserably. "I simply wanted to be near him, to love him and comfort him and help him through this terrible time. But I was afraid that if I revealed my true identity, Pierce wouldn't see me in that light."

"You did him a great disservice in assuming that."

"Perhaps, but I was in shock. It was all I could do keep myself together." Nicole looked up and found Alice's gaze on her, full of sympathy. "Tommy was my lifeline at a time when I badly needed one, and it didn't seem such a dreadful thing to offer to stand in as his nanny. Who was I hurting?"

"Yourself," Alice said. "And eventually, Pierce. I've known him a long time, Nicole. He won't take it well when he learns you've deceived him like this. He places great stock in honesty and trust."

Nicole blinked at the tears blinding her. "I don't need to hear this right now, Alice. Things are complicated enough."

"They can only get worse, my dear." She gestured at Nicole's head. "As I mentioned the first time we met, the hair threw me at first—you're so dark and Arlene was a natural blond. That distracts a person initially, but the closer I look, the more I see similarities. The shape of your mouth, your smile—they're what give you away to an observant eye, and I'm amazed I'm the only one to have noticed."

"You think Pierce might?"

"He might not. Until his accident, he was overseas a lot of the time and didn't see that much of Arlene or get to know her all that well. But someone else will, in time. Especially after tonight when so many people who did know her saw you for the first time."

She gripped both of Nicole's hands. "Take my advice, and tell Pierce before someone else does. Please, Nicole."

"I want to, but—"

The rustle of taffeta at the door alerted both women to another presence seconds before Louise's voice floated silkily across the room. "So sorry to interrupt, but I wondered if I might borrow an emery board." She held up one elegant hand and waggled the forefinger. "I broke a nail and it's driving me mad."

"I'm surprised you don't carry one with you," Alice

said, reaching into her own bag. "Here, use mine. Keep it, in fact. I have another, should I need it."

Aware of the incriminating evidence spread out between them, Nicole took advantage of Alice's actions to stuff the envelope and its contents under the love seat's cushions. Louise raised her eyebrows and gave a faint smile. "Dear me," she cooed, "did I interrupt something terribly private?"

"Not at all," Alice said smoothly. "We were merely looking at old family pictures."

She waited until the door had closed firmly in the wake of Louise's departure before resuming her seat. Her eyes were worried as she regarded Nicole. "You know what will happen if that woman finds out what's been going on and gets to Pierce before you do? She's itching for an excuse to discredit you in his eyes."

Nicole went cold. "You think she suspects?"

"Not who you really are, no, but only because she's too wrapped up in her own looks to pay particular notice to anyone else's and she was never close to Arlene. They shared nothing in common. But Louise is no fool and she's figured out that something's going on between you and Pierce. I don't pretend to know what it is and I'm not asking for any details. That's between you and him. But it's obvious to me that there's…"

"What?" Nicole asked, stunned at the insight of this unexpected ally.

Alice lifted her shoulders expressively. "Well, for want of a better word, let's say there's an attraction. If I've noticed, you can be certain Louise has, and I don't think I have to tell you that she'll make a very bad enemy, Nicole. Don't expect her to show any mercy, if she gets hold of this information before Pierce does."

"But nothing's going on between me and Pierce," Nicole said. Nor was it. They'd both agreed on that.

Alice leaned back against the love seat cushions and rolled her eyes. "Of course it is! He tracks your every move and you—" She laughed softly and reached forward to embrace Nicole in a hug. ''Your feelings are written all over your face as plain as day. You're in love with him and you've not done nearly as good a job of hiding that as you have of covering up who you really are.''

''I'm not good at keeping secrets,'' Nicole said miserably. ''I hate all the subterfuge.''

''Well, you're keeping one too many, my dear. Don't let Louise be the one to bare it, Nicole. If you and Pierce are to find any sort of future together, romantic or otherwise, he has to hear the truth from you and it's my guess you don't have a lot of time in which to do it. Tell him tonight, before it's too late.''

CHAPTER SEVEN

THE party went on for hours. Long after Alice had gone home and Tommy was soundly asleep, the music played, the people stayed, and Nicole's nerves grew increasingly frazzled. Afraid that if she waited for Pierce in the library as planned, someone else might spot her resemblance to Arlene, she went instead to the southeast side of the house, to the deck outside the kitchen.

Flinging a sweater over her shoulders to ward off the night chill, she sat at the small table where she and Janet so often enjoyed morning coffee together. The air was full of the scent of summer; of flowers and raspberries and rosemary. Out there, the music was swallowed up by the bulk of the house, no more than a pale accompaniment to the lazy whisper of the ocean creeping up the wide, deserted beach.

She would be hard-pressed to come by a more peaceful scene and oh, her soul craved a little peace! But the jagged edges of grief which she thought had begun to heal had torn open again as a result of her conversation with Alice.

All she could think was that she should have been sharing this tranquil moment with her sister. They should have been sitting there together, their connection something to be celebrated, not kept hidden like a shameful secret.

Tears, of sadness, of frustration, filmed her eyes. She wanted to shake her fist at the universe and scream her disappointment. It wasn't fair, none of it! Not the waste or the loss or the lies, and most of all not the cruelty of a child being robbed of his parents.

A beam of light from behind startled her into swinging

'round. Pierce stood profiled in the kitchen doorway. "I saw you heading this way. Mind if I join you now instead of waiting for later? Things are winding down inside and no one's going to miss me."

She shrugged. "I'm not very good company right now."

He caught the gleam of tears before she could blink them away. "Crying on such a beautiful night, Nicole? What's wrong?"

She turned away from him and watched the lacy froth of surf rolling ashore. "I was just thinking how much Tommy's mother is missing and wishing she could have been here tonight to see how beautifully he's growing up."

"Maybe she is. Who knows how wide or narrow the boundary is between life and death?"

The observation surprised her, betraying in him a dimension of sensitivity she'd not previously suspected. "Do you believe in an afterlife, Pierce?"

Pulling up the other chair, he sat down and tugged the knot in his tie loose. "There was a time I'd have said, no, it's once around the merry-go-round and that's it," he said, undoing the top button of his shirt. "But I'm not so sure anymore. Sometimes I..." He shook his head and rubbed a weary hand over his face. "Hell, I don't know what I'm trying to say except that Tom's father and I were very close and it's hard to let go the connection. We grew up together, went to the same schools, belonged to the same clubs. We even dated the same girls once in a while."

It was hard to picture that young, carefree person. Her impressions of Pierce were too caught up in the present image of a man picking up the pieces of a life thrown into disarray and making it work despite everything. "Didn't those girls mind being passed back and forth between you?"

"Probably. The point I'm trying to make, though, is that Jim and I shared so much in common. Even after I joined the Navy and wasn't around much anymore, the bond remained strong. When I was discharged, we picked up exactly where we'd left off, even though he was married by then.''

It was a risky question but Nicole couldn't help asking, ''What was his wife like?''

''She was a gem. Very calm and capable.'' He looked up again and his next remark shot arrows of terror in Nicole's heart. ''A lot like you, in some ways.''

''Like me?'' Consternation left her voice high-pitched and foreign-sounding to her ears but Pierce appeared not to notice.

''Uh-huh. Good with Tom. Never too busy or too tired to play with him or read to him, from what I could see—not that I ever spent that much time around her except for the last few months. But even from our limited acquaintance, it was clear that she was crazy about Jim. In some ways, it was as well they were both killed because I don't know that either of them could have survived losing the other.''

Nicole pressed her lips together and looked away, envying him his acceptance of a tragedy it sometimes seemed she herself would never come to terms with.

''The weird thing is,'' Pierce went on, leaning back in his chair and staring at up the stars, ''I sometimes feel Jim's presence. Or maybe it's just wishful thinking.'' He shook his head. ''I don't know. What about you? Do you believe in life after death?''

''I want to,'' Nicole whispered. ''I want to more than just about anything. But like you, I have doubts. I *do* know that families can draw comfort from each other in times of loss, and that no one, especially not a child, can have too many relatives to fill the void left by a parent's death.''

She drew a shaky breath at the realization that, without exactly planning it, she'd brought the conversation around to give herself the perfect opening for what she knew she must tell him. Quickly, before her courage evaporated, she went on, "Pierce, there's something I need to talk to you about."

"I'm listening," he said encouragingly when, after getting past the initial hurdle, she lapsed into silence.

She pressed the fingertips of her left hand to her lips and closed her eyes for a second, willing the right words to come to her. But that was to wish for a miracle because there was no way to make her lies right. They had been wrong from the first and all she'd done by allowing them to continue was compound them.

Still, she tried. "The reason I came to Morningside— the reason I left Rochester—I told you it was that I needed a change. That wasn't exactly true."

Not *exactly?* It had been a bare-faced lie, the first of too many! "Actually, I gave up my job..."

When she faltered again, Pierce sat erect and swiveled around in his chair to face her. "For God's sake, Nicole, don't tell me you think you made a mistake in coming here and—"

"I'm afraid I did, Pierce."

But he rushed on, overriding her interruption. "No! Look, I realize that looking after a healthy four-year-old must seem like a waste of your talent. Obviously, it's not as challenging as caring for critically sick children, but Tom needs you, Nicole. If you leave us now, I don't know how he'll cope—another loss, so soon after the accident, it would be too much. He'll miss you—we both will."

"It's not that I want to leave," she said.

"What, then? Money? Is that it? Do you need extra money? Name your price—anything you want. More time off?" More agitated than she'd ever seen him, he raked at his hair. "I know you put in long hours, but I thought you wanted it that way. When I've suggested you visit your relatives—"

"It's not about money!" she cried. "You keep bringing that up as if *it* counts more than...than *feelings*. But you can't put a price on a child's happiness. You can't buy love. And it's not about time off, either. A child is an around-the-clock responsibility and the most rewarding job in the world.''

"Then I don't understand." He reared back and when he spoke again, his voice was dark with sudden suspicion. "Is it me? Am I such a difficult man to live with, Nicole?''

"It's not about you," she said, struggling to complete what she'd started. Her true connection to Tommy presented problems enough, without her trying to navigate the minefield of her feelings for Pierce Warner.

"I think it is," he said, confronting her with that direct stare that never failed to shame her with its candor. "I think that whatever is troubling you has everything to do with us, with you and me and what happened between us last—''

Another shadow blocked the light still streaming from the kitchen doorway. "Pierce, sweetie, is that you hiding out there in the dark?''

"Son of a bitch!" he cursed under his breath, yanking savagely at his tie.

"Who's that you're talking to, Pierce?" Louise stepped out onto the deck and peered into the shadows. "Oh, it's you, Miss Bennett. I didn't realize you'd decided to put in another appearance again after your little tête-à-tête with Mrs. Holt.''

Pierce stood up but kept his back turned on Louise. "I want to finish this," he muttered to Nicole. "Whatever's bothering you, let's get it out in the open and deal with it. I'd like to think you trust me enough to be honest with me, Nicole, just as I intend to be with you. Because there's something I want to say to you, too—but not here. We need to go someplace where we won't be overheard or interrupted. If I arrange it, will you come away with me tomorrow—take a few hours off so we can get everything sorted out between us?''

It was the most tempting offer of her life, except... "But who'll look after Tommy?''

"I'll ask Janet. She's mentioned often enough that she'd be glad to stand in occasionally so that you can take time for yourself."

"Then, yes, I'll go with you," Nicole breathed, capitulating without another moment's hesitation. Because he was absolutely right; they did need some seclusion and privacy. Trying to unburden herself here, with the constant threat of interruption, was impossible. She couldn't just spit out the bald facts and be done with them. She needed time to explain her reasons, to justify her deceit. And who knew? Perhaps, when all was said and done, he'd understand and they could start over with no secrets between them. Or better yet, perhaps they could take up where they'd left off, that night by the pool, and write a different ending.

He closed his fingers briefly around her wrist. "Then I'll arrange it."

Louise approached, stiletto heels rapping a staccato rebuke on the cedar decking. "Am I intruding on a private moment?" she inquired, the question larded with cool suspicion.

"Not in the least." Jaw rigid with exasperation, Pierce swung around to face her. "Are the last guests leaving finally?"

"Oh dear, have you found the evening *such* a dreadful bore, sweets?"

"I wouldn't go that far," Pierce replied, and Nicole knew, from the way his voice faded, that Louise was drawing him back toward the house, "but it's been a long day and I'm about ready to call it quits."

"Then my timing's perfect because I came to tell you the Camerons are waiting to say good night and so are the Wileys. Once they're gone, you and I can put our feet up, enjoy a nightcap and talk. So much happened tonight, Pierce, some very strange and interesting incidents...."

Indeed yes! And topping the list, her discovering the nanny deep in secretive conversation in her private suite

with a guest who, presumably, was a complete stranger
to her. Like a bloodhound on the scent, Louise had
picked up on the fact that Nicole was hiding something.
It was a matter of time only before she found out what.

Tomorrow's date with Pierce couldn't have come at a
more fortuitous time.

It was past midnight when he turned out the last lamp
and climbed the stairs. By then, Nicole's door was
closed and her room in darkness which was probably
just as well. Given half a chance, he'd have been in there
with her and doing his damnedest to get her into bed
with him, which was hardly the best way to convince
her that it was more than her body that interested him.

The fact was, he was bewitched by her, obsessed by
her. Hell, why pussyfoot around the issue; he was in love
with her! And after tonight's aborted conversation, he
was terrified she was about to walk out of his life.

He didn't like that feeling one little bit. He wasn't
used to not being in charge—of himself and everyone
else. Yet instinct told him he was, to coin a phrase, in
well over his head when it came to the woman whose
only role had supposedly been to fill the gaps left in
Tom's life. He'd had no idea that his own was equally
full of holes, albeit it of a different kind, until tonight.

This lovely, gentle woman had walked into his life
when he most needed her and he'd been too blind to
recognize it. Not someone given to complicating his life
unnecessarily, he prided himself on facing reality head-
on. He took for granted his intelligence, his capability,
much as he took for granted that he was six foot two
and had blue eyes, yet where she was concerned, he'd
been about as stupid as a one-eyed drunken sailor trying
to fathom which end of a gangplank led to shore.

Ironically, it had taken a showdown with Louise to
jolt him into accepting what any other fool would have
recognized weeks ago, confronting his true state of mind.
Admittedly, he'd been blindsided by his feelings for

Nicole but, if he'd used a grain of sense, he'd have realized something serious was afoot when his sexual interest in Louise died so suddenly and irrevocably.

Instead, he'd done what so many of his men used to do when they'd learned of a relationship going sour: refused to deal with it and hoped that it would simply go away without his having to get in the thick of things. He'd compensated for his lack of romantic interest in Louise by allowing her undue latitude in other aspects of his life which, in turn, had culminated in today's ridiculous social charade.

He'd hated having strangers prowling all over his house, people with whom he had only a nodding acquaintance and little in common. He'd resented her proprietary air toward him and his home; resented even more her thinly-disguised aversion to Tom which she was finding increasingly difficult to hide.

He'd barely been able to wait for everyone to be gone, for the front door to shut behind them all, and for the household to settle back into the rhythm he'd come to love. But as if she sensed something untoward in the works, Louise had lingered, pointedly ignoring his less than subtle remarks on the late hour.

"My feet," she'd declared, kicking off her shoes, "are killing me. Pour me a brandy, sweetie."

"Why? Will it help your feet?" he hadn't been able to resist asking.

She'd laughed—or at least, she affected amusement. He'd begun to see that affectation was as much a part of her as her hazel eyes and long lovely legs. Take them away and there'd be only a shell left behind. A more tolerant man would have viewed that as a pity, but tonight had pushed him beyond the point of such generosity.

"Silly!" she'd chirped. "Of course not. But it would be a lovely way to end the day, don't you think? Just you and I alone like this?" She'd sighed and gazed around the room fondly. "I feel so at home here, Pierce. This is my kind of house."

"Oh?" he'd said guardedly, knowing well enough that she thought the decor too stuffy and his desk too untidy. "How so? It's nothing like your place, which I thought was exactly what you wanted."

"My place is perfect for a single, career-oriented woman, but this..." She'd waved expansively. "Sweetie, *this* is a family home. The floor plan here is perfect, with its nursery quarters and kitchen wing quite separate from the formal elegance of the reception rooms. It's so important, don't you think, that children have a place where they can be themselves without being underfoot all the time?"

"More to the point, Louise, is that I've come to enjoy having Tom underfoot, whereas you...."

She'd read criticism in his remark and sprung up from her chair agitatedly. "I'm doing my best, Pierce! It's not as if he's really your child, after all."

"I'm not blaming you," he'd said quietly. "Not everyone is cut out for parenting." He'd shrugged, still mystified at the way the role had crept up on him and taken such a strong hold. "Heck, if you'd asked me six months ago how I felt about the idea, I'd have said 'Not much.'"

"Well, there you are, then! Let's talk about something more agreeable, such as how we're going to spend tomorrow. The weatherman's predicting a gorgeous day again so how about an early round of golf before it gets too hot?"

"I'm afraid not. I've made other plans."

"And they'll take all day?"

"Probably."

"And tomorrow night? Will I see you then?"

"No," he said gently. "I don't think so, Louise."

He'd felt like a piece of dirt at the look that crept into her eyes at that. Suddenly, she wasn't the sharp-edged Realtor who'd negotiated the purchase of his house and supervised most of its new decor, she was merely a woman unable to hide her hurt or disappointment at having her expectations dashed.

He'd realized then that he couldn't allow things to drift any longer. Not only was it unfair to her, it was cowardly of him. The time had come to speak plainly. He drew in a sharp breath, searching for the best, the kindest way, to tell her.

But something in his expression must have spoken for him because she surprised him by saying, "It's over between us, isn't it, Pierce? It's been over for quite some time."

"Yes," he said, meeting her gaze levelly.

"And there's someone else, isn't there?"

Oh, brother! Peacekeeping in the Persian Gulf had been a piece of cake compared to this! "Yes."

"The nanny."

Good grief, were all women clairvoyant? Could Nicole see through him as easily? Was he going to spend the rest of his life having his wife tell him his secrets before he knew them himself?

Surprisingly, the idea didn't dismay him the way it once would have. In fact, he found the notion rather captivating.

"Well," Louise said, some of her usual acerbity starching her voice again, "I guess I just got my answer."

He came uncomfortably close to blushing. "I didn't—"

"You didn't have to, Pierce. The look on your face said it all." She eyed him narrowly. "Tell me, how much do you really know about Miss Nicole Bennett?"

"Enough," he said.

"Really? Were you aware that she was acquainted with Alice Holt before tonight?"

"I knew she had family in the area."

"That's hardly the same thing."

"Nicole isn't relevant to this discussion, Louise," he said wearily.

"If she's the reason you're dumping me, I don't agree."

He'd known then that it was time to bring the conversation to an end. He'd had no wish to inflict more pain but the last remark left him with little choice. "She isn't. You and I rushed too quickly into an affair that was ill-advised for all that it was briefly enjoyable. I regret it now and I'm sorry if I've hurt you."

"Worry about hurting yourself, darling," she said with a brittle smile, sliding her feet into her elegant shoes. "There's something altogether very fishy about Nicole Bennett and I'd hate to see her smash your illusions of happy-ever-after."

"I can take care of myself."

"Don't be so sure of that, Pierce. Love makes fools of the best of us."

She'd left then, and if it was possible for a man to feel even lower than dirt, he did. At the same time, however, he knew a wonderful sense of freedom and anticipation for tomorrow.

For the first time since he'd been forcibly retired from active service, he had a clear sense of exactly where he wanted his life to go. He could only pray that Nicole was willing to travel the same road.

He took her to his old family cottage on Lake Finlay. "A place where we can be alone, with nothing and no one to distract us," he said, heading the car along the inland highway which led to a range of low foothills rising in the east.

It was a perfect summer morning, the only clouds being those clustering on Nicole's private horizon. But before the day was over, she would tell him everything. She had to; the burden of her deceit was becoming too heavy to bear.

"I haven't seen the place in years and it's probably

more rundown than I remember it.'' Settling into the car's deep leather upholstery, Pierce angled a smile her way and slung his arm casually over the back of the seat so that his fingers rested mere inches from her neck. In khaki shorts and a white polo shirt, he looked more handsome than the law allowed; strong-limbed, lithe and muscular.

Briefly, she closed her eyes and wondered if he'd still be smiling at her by the day's end. Or would his eyes have turned cold, his mouth bitter?

"Jim and I spent every summer up there when we were kids and loved it,'' he went on, undeterred by her lack of response.

Then don't take me there today, she wanted to cry out. *I don't want to spoil your memories with my ugly confession.*

Her scalp prickled with awareness at the proximity of his hand. She ached to have him touch her, a bone-deep longing that made what she had to tell him that much harder to face. If only she'd been honest from the start…!

"Wait 'til you see the lake, Nicole. The water's clear as glass and warm as a bath.''

Wait 'til you hear what I have to tell you, she thought miserably. *You'll probably wish I'd drown in it.* "You obviously love it.''

"Yeah. It holds nothing but good memories for me.''

Blithely unaware of her distress, Pierce continued to regale her with stories from his past as the miles spun by. At length they turned off the main highway and traveled north along a narrow country road. The scenery was breathtaking, but Nicole was in no mood to enjoy it. Her mind was too occupied with the dilemmas confronting her.

When would be the best time to tell him? How would she begin? Should she have brought all the documentation to prove her real identity? The questions hammered at her without mercy.

"Did you remember to bring your swimsuit?" he asked, stepping on the accelerator to pass a slow-moving farm vehicle.

"Since you made a point of asking me to, yes, I did."

She'd debated long and hard over the wisdom of doing so. Tempting fate a second time hardly seemed smart in light of the last time she and Pierce had swum together. Eventually, though, she'd decided that, in light of the disclosures she planned to make before the day was out, it probably wouldn't matter if she paraded around in nothing but a G-string. It was unlikely he was going to show any interest in making love to her again, once he knew she'd wormed herself into his household under false pretenses.

Eleven-thirty came and went. "How much farther do we have to go?" she asked, feeling more and more like a prisoner soon to meet his executioner. The tension was unbearable. Every nerve in her body screamed for her to face up to things now and get matters over with, one way or the other. A quick death was preferable to this lingering agony.

"About another fifty miles. We'll be there in time for lunch. You might have noticed the hamper Janet packed—there's enough food to feed a whole fleet."

Less than an hour to bare her soul...not enough time, after all. She couldn't just leap into explanations and excuses without warning. Better to wait until they arrived, instead of distracting his attention from the twisting narrow road. Her news would surely hit him like a bombshell and just because her own life was on the skids was no reason to jeopardize his.

The time flew by, racing her closer to a disaster she could find no way to avert. "Tell me about your childhood," he suggested at one point.

Now! her guilty conscience screamed. *You wanted the perfect opening and he just gave it to you. Tell him now, before the chance slips away.*

"What's the matter? Did I just resurrect a ghost?"

His smile was warm and funny and gorgeous, his eyes the same unclouded blue as the sky. How could she destroy such a moment? Even without the altogether unforgivable fact of her deceit, this wasn't the time to rain down the unfortunate details of her early childhood.

"No," she said, feigning a yawn, "but the sun's making me dopey."

"Then take a nap," he said. "The story of your life can go on hold for now."

Would that it could wait forever!

He slid his arm around her and pulled her toward him so that her head rested against his shoulder. The connection, alive though it was with undercurrents of sexuality, ran to something more enduring which had begun to take shape days, weeks, before. Something that had begun with respect and grown into liking and from there had flowed like a stream, finding its way with unerring instinct to the sea, growing deeper and stronger and more certain with each passing mile.

And now it was in full flood and she was being swept along, helpless to extricate herself or him from its hold.

What she wouldn't have given at that moment to turn back the tide! If only she'd known, the day she walked into his house, that he was the man she'd come to love more dearly than life, how differently might she have handled matters!

The next time he spoke, it was to tell her they'd arrived at the cottage. He parked the car at the end of a rutted dirt driveway overhung with evergreens through which the sun filtered in lazy golden beams. Beyond, lichen-covered rocks sloped gently down toward a white-painted house perched on the tip of the small promontory, with the lake a vivid sweep of blue below.

"Well, this is it," he said, giving her shoulders a squeeze. "The place that holds so many good memories for me. And in case you're wondering, you're the only woman I've ever brought up here. I hope you realize how special that makes you."

CHAPTER EIGHT

THE interior of the cottage was a delight, a mélange of antique and white wicker furniture, old pine floors, exposed beams and sunny yellow walls covered with original watercolors. A floor-to-ceiling stone fireplace dominated one wall of the living room, with paned windows which looked out across the lake filling the one next to it.

Using his shoulder for extra leverage, Pierce forced open a pair of French doors which apparently hadn't been used in some time. "There's a nice old-fashioned porch out here where the grandmothers used to sit in their rockers and enjoy their afternoon tea. It might be a nice place to have lunch, though I wouldn't mind going down for a swim first. How about you?"

The heat was much more intense this far inland. Her cotton top and shorts stuck to her skin and a film of perspiration dotted her upper lip. "It sounds heavenly."

"Grab your stuff then, and I'll show you where you can change." He dusted off one palm against the other and led the way up a narrow twisting staircase.

The were two bedrooms, each containing two double bedsteads with iron frames painted white, and thick mattresses piled high with handmade quilts and feather pillows. In both rooms, windows matching those in the living room looked out across the lake.

"Going to bed here was never a problem, even when we were kids," Pierce remarked, coming to stand behind her and pulling her back to lean against him as they both gazed out at the view. "We'd lie awake listening to the loons, the coyotes would sing, and the moon would turn the lake into a sheet of silver. Jim and I would lie crosswise on the bed and stare out at the stars and plan what we'd do the next day. Our biggest dream was to find the stash of gold which legend says the mountain man who built the original house buried somewhere close by so that hostile Indians wouldn't get it.''

''Tommy will dream the same dreams, one day, I imagine,'' Nicole said.

His sigh was full of regret. ''But he won't have his father around to tell him how it used to be.''

''He'll have you, Pierce.'' *And me, God willing.* ''Have you never brought him here?''

''No, but Jim and Arlene did. They loved the cottage and had already spent several weekends here this year, before…well, before. That's why everything's up and running and ready to be used after being shut down for the winter. Come to think of it, there are probably still some of their clothes and stuff in the closets. I guess I should clear them out, but not today.'' He rubbed his chin on her head. ''Today is just for us.''

So why spoil it with confessions any sooner than she had to, Nicole asked herself, reveling in the strength of his arms around her. She'd kept quiet this long. What real difference were a few more hours going to make?

He relaxed his hold just enough to turn her around to face him and she knew he was going to kiss her. Was it selfish of her to let him? To take what he was so willing to give her? If they cemented the bond between them with moments like this, might it not help, later, when she explained to him who she really was? Because without anything specific having yet been said, they'd somehow found a firm footing on the level they'd skirted for so long; one which placed them securely in the realm of lovers.

And lovers forgave one another…didn't they?

His mouth was hungry, slanting across hers, taking possession of its most guarded secrets, and stirring her to a depth of wanting that eclipsed anything but the need to become a part of him for however long he'd let her.

The bed was at her back, beckoning, and she more than willing to avail herself of its welcome.

But he was not. "I'm getting ahead of myself," he said hoarsely, putting her from him and backing out of the door. "Hurry up and get changed before my whole game plan goes down the tubes."

When she came downstairs, he had carried their picnic basket out to the porch and was in the process of unloading its contents. Already in swimming trunks, he looked, Nicole thought, more delicious than anything the hamper could possibly produce.

"Just as I suspected, Janet did pack enough food to feed a squadron," he complained good-naturedly. "I phoned her while you were changing, by the way, just to make sure she was coping okay with Tom. Seems they're having a great day making chocolate cake and cookies, and keeping Peaches out of mischief."

"I'm glad," Nicole said, spreading a red linen cloth over the table and laying out cutlery and plates. "I felt guilty leaving her in charge of him when I know how much else she has to do, but I wouldn't have felt easy leaving Tommy with a stranger."

"And she wouldn't have allowed it even if you had. She's very fond of you, you know, and took me severely to task last night when I mentioned coming up here with you."

He shook a loaf of French bread reprovingly and in an atrocious imitation of Janet who was given to somewhat high-pitched annoyance, recited, "'That girl hasn't had a real break from her job since she started here in May, Pierce Warner, and I was beginning to wonder if you'd ever notice that she's driving herself into the ground without a word or gesture of gratitude from you. Your mother, God rest her soul, would be scandalized! It's high time you came to your senses.'"

"And you survived all that?" Although she was laughing, Nicole knew Janet had a sharp tongue on occasion and apparently had chosen to use it on Pierce.

"I'm here to talk about it, aren't I?"

"I was hoping you were here because you wanted to be," she said boldly. "I was under the mistaken impression it was your idea to bring me here for the day, not Janet's."

"Oh, it was my idea," he assured her, his gaze roaming possessively over her. "I wasn't about to let anything deter me from that, sweetheart, but it's nice to know I've got Janet's blessing because she can be a devil to deal with if she's crossed."

Sweetheart...he'd called her *sweetheart!* A delicious heat flushed through her that owed nothing to diffidence and a very great deal to the molten hunger for him that flowed restlessly through her blood.

"She also pointed out," Pierce continued, unearthing smoked trout mousse and crackers, pâté, green olives and seedless black grapes, thinly sliced breast of chicken and lemon tarts, "that you were 'a prize worth keeping' in case I hadn't noticed." His hands grew still around the neck of a bottle of white wine, and nothing but the muted thunder of Nicole's heart filled the small silence that followed.

At length, she ventured a glance at him. "And what did you say to that?"

"That I agreed with her entirely. Nicole, I didn't bring you here today just for a break in routine. I wanted to have you here, in a place that holds such special memories, because there's something I need to ask you."

Stuffing the wine bottle into a clay cooler, he came around the table and, taking her hand, pulled her down on the glider swing at the end of the porch. "You and I have talked endlessly about the best way to bring up Tom, about values and morals, about preschool and kindergarten and whether or not a child should watch television. But we've never really talked honestly about us. About a man and a woman powerfully drawn to one another. I've kissed you and made love to you, against my better judgment and yours perhaps, but I've never told you how I feel about you. I don't think I knew myself—or else I wasn't ready to admit it—until last night when I suddenly had the most godawful feeling that I was about to lose you. And I realized at that moment that it wouldn't just leave a hole in Tom's life if you weren't here, but that mine would be..." He lifted his shoulders helplessly, searching for words. "Mine," he said, looking deep into her eyes, "would be so bloody empty and unbearable that I don't know how I'd manage. And this is the longest speech I've ever made in my life, so will you please shut me up by saying something?"

She gazed back at him, unable to speak for the lump in her throat and with her eyes swimming with tears.

"Oh, hell!" he murmured, crushing her to him. "I didn't mean to make you cry. Is it what I've said? Have I spoken too soon?"

She shook her head. "No. You've said exactly the right thing. It's just that I'm not sure what it will mean when—"

"I'm trying to tell you I love you," he cut in anxiously. "I'm not suggesting some sort of clandestine affair or an occasional date. I'm asking you if you'll marry me and doing a lousy job of it, by the looks of things."

"But you can't do that," she cried. "Not yet. You don't know enough about me."

"I know all I need to know." He buried his face in her hair, trailed kisses over her eyelids and along her cheekbone. "I know that you love Tom and that having him as a permanent part of our life together won't be a problem for you."

"Oh, never," she whispered, placing her hands flat against the solid planes of his chest and drowning in his gaze. "I do love him, Pierce, I really do. But I want you to know that I love you, too, and I wish—I wish I hadn't waited until now to tell you something you had the right to know long before now—"

"The time had to be right for both of us," he said,

misunderstanding. "And how could you be expected to say anything with Louise an unresolved issue between us?"

She could feel his heart hammering beneath her palm; felt her own leap into frenzied response at the naked hunger she saw reflected in his eyes. She was lost then, caring for nothing but the urge to answer his need in the only way that would assuage them both.

Taking his hand, she drew it to her left breast and let him discover for himself she, too, walked a very fine line between control and the fury of a passion she'd never before experienced. "If I were to die now," she said, the words overlaid with husky emotion, "I would do so happy in the knowledge that I was in your arms and that, with my last breath, I told you again how much I love you."

He was the strongest man she'd ever known; the most honorable, the most fearless. But in that moment she almost had him reduced to tears. "I do not deserve you," he muttered, grazing his fingers over her flesh in wonder.

"You deserve much, much more," she said, her own hands loving him, loving the texture of his smooth, tanned skin, the sleek musculature of his torso, the vibrant thrust of his arousal against her thigh as he leaned over her.

Shame on you, her conscience cried. *Stop this now, before you damn yourself to eternity!*

But she could not. This might be her last chance at the only heaven she ever wanted to know. "Make love to me, Pierce," she begged. "Make me forget there is such a thing as sorrow and ugliness in the world."

A groan tore loose from his throat, a sound poised midway between pain and pleasure. He slid his hand over the slope of her breast, down her ribs and past the indentation of her waist, in a gesture of pure masculine possession. "I was so afraid I was losing you," he murmured. "Last night, you were slipping away from me and I didn't know how—"

"Don't talk about last night," she whispered, bringing his mouth back to hers and coercing him with quick, frantic kisses. "Nothing matters but this day, now...you and me..."

"Yes," he said, his eyes scouring her face, feature by feature. "Yes!"

He took her then, on the cushions of the old glider swing which swayed beneath them, cradling them as securely and lovingly as a mother. Unashamedly naked under the benevolent sun, with the sturdy old cottage as witness, he cradled her hips and lifted her to meet the proud thrust of his flesh.

She wanted to hold him within her forever, to retain the heat of his passion, the tangible reality of a coming together that transcended the merely physical. For the first time since she'd learned of her sister's death—perhaps for the first time in her entire life—she felt complete.

And justified. In everything she'd done. Because how could something so utterly beautiful have sprung from evil or wrongdoing? How could hearts so full of love possibly find room for anger or hatred? And how could anything hurt them as long as they shared such a perfect unity of body and soul?

But she could not keep him forever. She could not even keep herself. The greed was too voracious, the need too acute. Neither would be appeased by anything less than the destruction of the miracle it had created. Hearts' desire, souls' need, they meant nothing when it came to the satisfaction of the flesh.

Savagely it grabbed control, remorseless in its determination, reckless in its devastation. She felt herself dissolving around Pierce, disappearing into an ever-narrowing whirlpool. Then, too briefly, recovering, clinging.

She squeezed shut her eyes as though doing so would

somehow lessen the tension and appease the tremors within that threatened to destroy her. She knew from his tortured breathing that Pierce fought the same demons; that he, too, had no hope of defeating them.

Dazed, she ventured a glance at him. He hovered above her, staring at her, devouring her with his gaze. Searching out her soul as if it alone could save him from annihilation. A vein pulsed at his temple. The sweat stood out on his brow.

She moved, wrapping her legs tightly around his waist, her hands clutching at him, wanting to take all of him inside her. And in doing so, she brought about their destruction.

His pupils widened and a great breath filled his lungs. He lowered his head to hers. "Now," he whispered, burying his face in her hair. "Now!"

And the torment peaked, a fomentation that blasted them into extinction, and left them weightless and invincible for a few sweet seconds before allowing them to drift down again to become, once more, hostage of their private fears and secrets.

They made love two more times that afternoon, once after lunch when he caught her coming down the stairs where she'd gone to get her towel. He blocked her passage and stalked her back up to the bedrooms, choosing one at random and lifting her to the deep, soft mattress. Their kisses, that time, tasted of wine and bittersweet chocolate.

And love. "I love you," he told her, over and over.

He took her breath away. Whatever the price for this stolen day, she thought, dazed and sated, it was worth it. However many the disappointments in her future, the memories she and this extraordinary, wonderful man were creating today would remain clear and bright, untouched by regret. This simple cottage on the shores of a lake so calm it might have been made of glass would provide the setting for the one honest thing she could give Pierce Warner: her heart.

And confession? It could come later, on the way home. All that mattered was that she fulfill the promise she'd made to herself to tell him before the day was out.

Eventually, they made it as far as the lake for the swim they'd been promising themselves ever since they'd arrived. The water was warm and smooth as cream lapping around them. They shed their clothes again, and frolicked naked in its clear depths.

After, as they lay on the boat dock drying off, Pierce reached for her hand and said, "You do know that I want to marry you, don't you, Nicole?"

Despite everything they'd shared so far that day, she had not expected a proposal. Just for a moment, her heart stopped, caught like a trapped animal between two predators, and she wanted nothing more than to stop the clock until she'd taken care of the wrongs she had to put right, then set time rolling again and pick up where he'd left off with the answer her heart longed to give.

"Nicole? Honey?" The pressure of his fingers increased. "Will you please say something?"

He didn't like the sudden stillness that spread over her. He didn't like the way her expression closed, shutting her off from him.

He cursed inwardly. He shouldn't have spat out the words quite like that or quite so soon but, hell! He couldn't imagine a better time. They'd never been closer, or the bond between them more sure. Yet the quality of her silence told him he'd somehow said the wrong thing.

Rolling over, he propped himself on one elbow and squinted at her. She immediately jackknifed to a sitting position and tried to turn away from him, but not quite soon enough to hide the gleam of tears on her lashes or the shadows chasing through her beautiful dark eyes.

"On second thought," he said, stunned by the dismay

that churned his insides to mush, "change that to, 'Say yes.' Or have I taken too much for granted?"

She stared out across the lake and said in a dead voice, "No. I would be honored to marry you."

He stared at the delicate line of her spine, the graceful way her shoulders bowed forward, as though to protect her from a blow. He'd never proposed before but it didn't take a whole lot of know-how to recognize there was something decidedly off about the way she was responding. A deliriously happy bride-to-be she was not.

He cleared his throat. "Good," he said, and drummed the tips of his fingers together.

Had he missed some vital step? Overlooked a crucial part of the ritual?

A ring, you fool!

He reached out to touch her, then changed his mind. She might have been carved from marble for all the life emanating from her. "Sweetheart," he said, "if this is all coming down on you too fast, just say the word. I've waited thirty-five years to find the woman I want to spend the rest of my life with. I can wait a few more days."

A shudder passed over her and he heard a gasp; a little sound quickly stifled but unmistakably drenched in sadness. He searched for the right thing to say: something tender, something loving, something to reassure her. "Oh, hell's bells!" he said.

He'd learned a lot during his stint in the Navy, not the least being that women weren't like men. What he hadn't learned was what to do when faced with those differences.

It seemed to him that if a woman loved a man, she'd be pretty happy when he asked her to marry him. It seemed equally clear that if she wasn't happy with his proposal, it could be only for one of two reasons: either she didn't love him enough, or else she was already married to some other guy.

"Is there someone else, Nicole?" he asked, not wanting to hear her say yes, but deciding that anything was better than the limbo he was presently enduring.

Limbo, nothing! He was in hell.

"No," she said in a muffled voice.

"But there's a problem?"

"Yes."

She was shaking so hard that all he wanted was to take her into his arms and tell her that he wouldn't let anything on earth stand between them. Nor would he, as long as... "Answer me one thing, then. Do you love me?"

"Yes!" she cried, swiveling around and leaning against him with the tears rolling down her face. "With all my heart, but—"

The crippling pain that had taken hold of his heart eased at that, and he found he could breathe again. "Then the 'buts' don't matter," he said, holding her close and rocking her back and forth. "At least, they don't matter today. Whatever it is, we'll sort it out tomorrow. All I want to hear today is that you'll marry me."

She lifted her face and wiped at the tears dribbling down her cheeks. "Pierce," she began.

"Either say you'll marry me, or else tell me to take a hike, Nicole. Because this is killing me."

She reached for his face, tracing the contour of his cheek, his jaw, and he didn't need to hear the words. They were there in her touch, her eyes, the soft curve of her mouth. "I'll marry you," she said. "I love you." And she kissed him.

He probably shouldn't have done what he did then, but sheer relief made him crazy. Like a man emerging from a near-death experience, he knew nothing but the need to lose himself in her softness yet again. To bury himself in the silken web of her femininity and never break free. To stamp her irrevocably with the mark of his possession. To renew himself in her.

On the porch, they had been driven by hunger. In the

bedroom he had made love to her the way a lover should: at leisure, with whispered words and quiet explorations; with awed appreciation for the beauty she brought not just to his senses but to his soul.

But there, with nothing but the weathered, sun-warmed planks of the dock and a thin cushioning of towel beneath them, he drove into her like a creature possessed. Fast and furious, spilling himself within her the way a man does when war threatens his mortality and he knows he might not live to see another sunset or another dawn.

He was ashamed after. Horrified to find the tear tracks still on her face. Shocked to see her mouth swollen from the force of his kisses. And most of all, devastated that when he tried, in his stupid, bumbling fashion, to comfort her, she clung to him and said over and over again that he had nothing to apologize for, that she was the one who should be sorry.

She was sorry? "Sweetheart," he murmured, his voice breaking like a teenager's. "Sweet, darling Nicole, I will honor and treasure you for the rest of my days." And couldn't say another damned word because his throat was too swollen with emotion.

She calmed down a bit after that. Enough that he was able to persuade her to go for another swim. Just a quiet drifting in the placid water to soothe the bruises in her heart.

To the north, a line of cloud advanced slowly, obscuring the blue. There'd be a storm before nightfall.

"Are you happy?" he dared to ask her, as they floated side by side and gazed up at the sky.

"Yes," she said, linking her fingers with his. "Are you?"

"More than I expected or dared to dream I'd be." The fear was gone, along with the uncertainty. He'd done the unimaginable: found the woman of his dreams and she'd agreed to be his wife. There was nothing on earth that could spoil that.

"Shall we pack up and head home?" he asked her. "Stop, maybe, on the way, and have dinner some-place?"

"That sounds lovely," she said listlessly.

The heat had been too much for her, he decided. It must have been close to a hundred degrees on the dock. Not a breath of wind stirred the trees, and the flowers Arlene had planted that spring wilted in the heat which shimmered in waves over the landscape.

Glancing up as they climbed the sun-baked rocks to the house, he saw that the sky overhead had assumed a metallic sheen that hurt the eyes. It was going to be one humdinger of a storm. Just as well they were moving out before it hit.

"Go change while I lock the place up and load the car," he said, when they reached the porch. "If I come up with you, we'll be here all night—which wouldn't be such a bad idea if it weren't that I promised Janet we'd be back today."

She was living a nightmare, the kind where something indescribably evil was closing in on her and no matter how fast she ran, she remained rooted to the spot. There was no escape; there was nothing but dread and fear and the knowledge that she was fated to meet a terrible end.

A tortoiseshell hairbrush lay on the dressing table next to one of the beds. Picking it up, she drew it slowly through her hair, watching the movement in the wavy old mirror. The woman staring back at her was a stranger. Solemn, remote, composed. A little flushed, perhaps, as if she'd had too much sun, but in control. No one would guess that, on the inside, she was falling apart.

She'd been so focused on her own agenda, it had never occurred to her that Pierce might have one, too; one which went beyond a simple day out at the lake.

Oh, spit out the truth for once! the remorseless voice

of conscience sneered. *You came up here all prepared for romance. You hoped he'd make love to you again.*

"But I didn't expect him to propose," she whimpered.

Of course you didn't. That sort of decent behavior is beyond your understanding.

"I intend to tell him."

When?

"Before the day's out."

She slammed the brush down, picked up her watch and fumbled with the clasp. Twenty-four minutes past five. She was running out of time.

What's keeping you from telling him right now?

The stranger in the mirror stared back, no longer composed. Her eyes glittered feverishly, her hands shook so badly the watch slipped and fell to the floor. She'd reached the end of her rope.

"No reason," Nicole said. "No reason at all."

Outside, a car door slammed, and then, oddly, another. Footsteps sounded, a light excited gait counterbalanced by Pierce's measured tread. The screen door creaked open.

"I can't imagine whatever it is being so important that you drove all the way up here to tell me about it." His words floated up the stairs, curt and unwelcoming.

"I didn't think this was something that could—or should wait," Louise Trent's unmistakable voice replied. "If the situation were reversed, God forbid, I'd certainly prefer to know as soon as possible."

I broke a fingernail and thought you might have an emery board I could borrow. The picture flashed into Nicole's mind: of her and Alice huddled together in her sitting room last night, the damning contents of that brown envelope spread out on the love seat between them; of her hastily stuffing them underneath the cushion at Louise's intrusion, then jumping up, the picture of guilt.

In the confusion that followed, she'd forgotten about them.

Had left them there, accessible to anyone who knew where to look for them. And Nicole knew with unerring certainty that they had been found.

Pierce was going to learn the extent of her duplicity not gently or kindly, with love and trust to cushion the blow, but swiftly, with malice and entirely without mercy. And she had no one but herself to blame for it.

CHAPTER NINE

LOUISE stood at the table, the incriminating envelope in her hand. It was the first thing Nicole saw as she came down the stairs and turned toward the dining room.

Pierce stood opposite, hands grasping the back of one of the chairs. His expression betrayed nothing but mild annoyance. "Louise," he said, quietly enough, "I think we said everything there was to say last night."

"I haven't come here to try to make you change your mind about me, Pierce," she said, turning the envelope over in her hands and stroking its edges with her thumbs. "It's the woman you think you do want that I'm trying to save you from. I respect you too much to let her make a fool of you."

The envelope drew Nicole like a magnet. Without volition, her feet carried her forward, into Pierce's line of vision, into Louise's.

"Save it, Louise," Pierce said. "I've asked Nicole to marry me and she's said yes. Nothing you have to say is going to change my mind about that."

Dark triumph blazing in her eyes, Louise flicked her gaze over Nicole, from her toes to her face and back to her toes again. "Are you so sure you know who your bride-to-be really is?"

"I know all I need to know. She's the woman I love."

"Ah, yes, the nanny! The dear, selfless little nurse who left such a prestigious hospital to come to a small west coast town and took a menial job looking after a child, just so she could be near her relatives." There was no missing the mockery in Louise's voice, the bright malice in her eyes. "Tell me, Pierce, how do you like her relatives?"

147

"I've never met them," he said, and for the first time, Nicole heard a note of uncertainty in his voice.

"But you have, sweets! You know one of them very, very well."

"Oh, for Pete's sake, stop talking in riddles!"

"All right, I'll come to the point." She raised the envelope and held it vertically at arm's length. "What I have in here might not be a picture, but it certainly speaks a thousand words."

"Give that to me!" Finding her voice at last, Nicole sprang forward, but too late.

Opening the flap of the envelope, Louise tipped the contents out on the table. Legal documents, letters, and the old dog-eared snapshot of two little girls interspersed with recent ones of Arlene with her husband and son, they all spilled out, evidence so damning, there was no denying it.

Still, and to his credit, Pierce tried, rejecting the collection with a dismissive gesture. "What is all this? And where did you get it?"

Nicole closed her eyes in despair at the shame burning her cheeks. "It's mine. She stole it from my room."

"And she's no more a nanny than I'm an astronaut!" Louise cried. "She's Tom's aunt. So forget any notions you have that she cares about you, Pierce, because you're nothing but an obstacle to what she's really after. She came here to Oregon and wheedled her way into your house for one reason only and that was to be near her nephew."

"Don't be ridiculous," he said. "You're either making this up or you've misunderstood."

Oh, my darling! Nicole wept silently, aching to touch him.

"No. Read it for yourself, if you don't believe me, Pierce. Go on!" With a sweep of her hand, Louise sent the papers skittering over the tabletop. "As your friend, I care too much to let you walk blindly into the trap she's set for you but if, when you find out why your precious Nicole really came to town, you can look me in the eye and tell me you still want to marry her, I'll not say another word.''

"You've said too much already," he returned heavily. "You had no business invading Nicole's privacy and you've accomplished nothing but to damage the friendship you claim to value so dearly."

Nicole lifted her head and stole a glance at him. He looked frozen, formidable, his features carved from stone. The urge to touch him died, just as his love for her was dying right before her eyes.

He spoke again. "If that's everything, Louise, I'd appreciate your leaving. Go home. There's nothing here for you."

The silence she left behind was unbearable, a great wall of glass about to shatter. When it did, Nicole knew its lethal shards would rip and tear at the fabric of everything lovely which she and Pierce had shared that day and leave it beyond any hope of repair.

"Pierce," she whispered, "it isn't the way Louise made it sound."

"Is there any truth at all to the accusations she's made?"

"Some. I am Tommy's aunt."

"I fail to see how you can be."

"Arlene was my sister. Our mother gave us up for adoption when we were small. Louise is right. It's all recorded here." She touched the jumble of papers with the tip of her finger.

As if he couldn't abide the sight of her, he paced into the living room and stared out of the windows. "Did you seriously think you could keep this a secret indefinitely?"

"No," she exclaimed. "It was never my intention to do that."

"Really! So when were you planning to reveal yourself?"

"Tonight," she said, despising the desperation she

heard in her voice. "I admit I've been putting it off, but I promised myself I'd tell you tonight at dinner."

"Why then? Because I'd already made such a fool of myself that another blow to my pride wouldn't kill me? Or did you really think that once you'd wrung a proposal out of me, I'd be too much the gentleman to renege on the offer?"

The first shard of pain found its mark. "Pierce, my relationship to Tommy has nothing to do with my feelings for you. You've got to believe that."

His laughter drove another sliver into her heart. "Give me one good reason why I should believe you'd tell me the correct time, let alone the truth. You've lied to me from the day you set foot in my house and done it so well, I never suspected a thing."

"I wanted to tell you right away," she cried.

"What stopped you, sweetheart? Your perverted sense of honor? Your nonexistent moral code?"

"I was afraid! I thought you'd see me as a threat to your custodial rights and refuse to let me near him. I'm Tommy's closest living relative, after all, and I didn't know anything about the kind of man you are."

"No, you didn't, but you didn't let that stop you from judging me and finding me wanting, did it?"

"You might have been jealous." How pitiful the reasons sounded, aired in the clear light of day. How self-serving and mean-spirited! "You might have thought I'd try to take him away from you."

"So you decided to become Mrs. Pierce Warner first. Pity Louise finessed your plan, isn't it?"

"I already told you, I was going to tell you everything tonight. I would never have married you with this secret between us, Pierce, never."

Desperate to make him understand the fear and grief that had driven her, she followed him into the living room. In the time since they'd come back to the cottage, the sky had grown ominously dark, adding an air of foreboding to an already somber scene.

Shivering despite the oppressive heat, she reached out to touch his shoulder, hoping to evoke something of the tenderness they'd shared earlier and in so doing, stir the embers of his sympathy, if not his understanding.

He didn't shrug her off so much as freeze her out. He was worse than immovable, he was unreachable. "Liar," he snarled, this man who, only an hour before, had told her he loved her and would cherish her the rest of his days.

"I am not lying now," she wept. "And I never lied about loving you. I want to spend the rest of my life with you, Pierce."

"Even if I decide that Tom is better off living with his grandparents in Arizona and that he'd visit us only once or twice a year? Would you still want me then, sweetheart?"

She couldn't bear the mockery with which he uttered the endearment. "Is it so terrible for me to want both of you?" she cried, yanking on his arm and pulling him around to face her. "In my place, wouldn't you? I went through most of my life not knowing I had a sister, then found her only to lose her again before I could see her, or hug her, or kiss her."

For a moment, she thought she'd penetrated the shell of rejection with which he'd armored himself against her. Just briefly, he met her gaze searchingly, before he swung back to the window.

"No, Pierce!" she exclaimed. "I won't let you turn away from me—from *us!* If my not wanting to chance losing contact with my sister's son makes me a despicable person in your eyes, at least have the guts to tell me so to my face."

"There's a bad storm coming," he said.

"I don't care if the world's about to end! I won't let you shut me out like this. I don't deserve it!"

"*You* don't deserve? Where the hell do you get off thinking you deserve a damn thing?"

"Even a criminal is entitled to a fair hearing," she

replied, stung. "Or is it still Navy practice to hang a man from the yardarm before he's had a chance to plead his case?"

He didn't reply. He seemed to find the view more engrossing than anything she could offer in her own defense. It was as if, having disappointed him in this one thing, she lacked credibility in every other respect, too.

"I hadn't figured you to be quite this petty," she said, too numbed by the hopes already dashed to pieces to care that she might be courting disaster with what was left of her dreams.

He flinched as the barb struck home. "If that's your opinion, I'm left to wonder why you were so ready to marry me—oh, but I forgot! Your acceptance of my proposal had nothing to do with me and everything to do with what you hoped to gain from such a convenient alliance."

"And you," she retorted, stirred to anger by his withering scorn, "are nothing but a spoilt brat who's decided to grab all his toys and go home because the game isn't being played exactly according to the rules he's set down. I made a mistake, I admit it, and I'm trying to set it right, but you aren't prepared to be forgiving."

Shaking her head, she turned back to the dining room. She'd fought to overcome her grief and disappointment over Arlene's death and thought she'd emerged the stronger for it. But the crushing effect of this latest blow sapped all the sweetness she'd found in Pierce's love and brought her face-to-face with her own frailty again.

"If what we feel for each other—the love we thought we shared—can't weather this, we'd have been in serious trouble down the road, Pierce."

"We're in serious trouble anyway," he said, and something in his tone sent alarm prickling over her.

"What do you mean by that?"

"Take a look."

Swiftly, she crossed the room to stand beside him again.

"See that peninsula halfway across the lake?" He pointed at a spit of land which stuck out at right angles to the eastern shore about a mile away. The previously calm surface of the water had changed, whipped into a rush of whitecaps which pounded the tip of the land.

Half an hour ago, houseboats had plied the calm waters, dinghies and runabouts had zipped back and forth between hidden coves and summer landings. Where were they now? "How could anyone survive out there?" she asked over the knot of fear in her throat.

"They couldn't," he said grimly. "That's a full-blown gale we're seeing, and it's headed our way."

The black line of cloud advanced toward the promontory on which the cottage stood, pushed at a furious rate by the wind already wreaking such havoc over the water.

"Oh, brother, this is bad!" Pierce scarcely breathed the words as the whitecaps churned into a froth of water that streaked the width of the lake, obliterating the spit and the far shore behind it.

And then, even as she watched, it suddenly whirled into a coiling mass and rose up into a perfectly formed funnel, exactly as if some giant straw had sucked it up toward the heavens.

The house was full of eerie shadows brought on by the premature twilight. Yet despite the lowering clouds, not a breath of wind stirred the leaves drooping limply from the trees. The world outside the cottage windows waited in unnatural stillness, as if the land was marshaling its troops to withstand the imminent onslaught approaching from the lake.

Out on the water, the funnel towered, gathering strength. Yet even when it began spinning toward the cottage, Nicole could barely tear her eyes away from the sight. It was awesome in its fury and the speed with which it ate up the distance.

"I think we'll be safer waiting this out under the dining room table," Pierce said, grabbing her wrist and

pulling her away from the window as the two hundred
foot pine that stood sentinel on the weather side of the
cottage rippled with advance warning. "That's a tornado
you're looking at and it could set this place on its beam
end."

Without ceremony, he hustled her out of the living
room and under the dining table, stopping only long
enough to open the back door before joining her. "To
give the wind an exit," he explained tersely when she
asked.

They were barely settled when the noise began, a low
keening that quickly rose to a scream.

"Here it comes," Pierce said, and the din was like
nothing Nicole had ever heard before, a horrible roaring,
like a house going up in flames with a person trapped
inside, shrieking for deliverance. At the same time, rain
pelted against the north wall, rattling the windows in
their frames.

Upstairs, one gave way before the onslaught, banging
open and thumping against the wall. Almost immediately after, another in the living room flew wide and
Pierce cursed. "The place will be flooded at this rate,"
he muttered. "These old windows weren't built to withstand this kind of attack. It's a miracle they've stood up
as long as they have."

And meanwhile, the tornado continued to rage.

Nicole had never been afraid of the weather before.
Even in Minnesota, where winter blizzards could cripple
the entire state in the space of an hour, she had never
known the utter helplessness that gripped her at that moment.

I'm going to die here, she thought, curling up against
Pierce and burrowing her face into his shoulder. *I'm
never going see my parents or Tommy again.*

Pierce couldn't get away from her. There was scarcely
room for the two of them under the table, even with his
legs and feet sticking out at one end, and he had little

choice but to slide his arm around her neck and cushion the back of her head with his hand.

"Hold on," he said, and whether he meant hold on to her courage, or hold on to him, she neither knew nor cared. She simply clung to him, shaking, and thought if her time had come, there was no way she'd rather go than in his arms.

But there was something she needed to say to him first. "I never meant to hurt you," she babbled, clutching a fistful of his shirtfront. "I didn't expect to fall in love with you and if I'd known I would, I'd have spoken much sooner, but things got away from me, Pierce. Every time I made up my mind to tell you, I'd look at Tommy—at us—and see a family shaping happiness from tragedy, and I couldn't bear to risk spoiling all that. But I love you with all my heart, I really do, and I want you to know that you've made these last days the most wonderful in my whole life."

And because he was so close and she couldn't help herself, she lifted her lips to his and kissed him. She hadn't meant it to last or flare into untrammeled passion. She just wanted to seal the words in some way; to let him know that she spoke from the heart.

At first, he resisted her but then, suddenly, he was kissing her back, fiercely, as if the holocaust outside had generated a storm in him that blasted his antipathy into oblivion.

His hands tangled in her hair, his mouth crushed hers, and for a few sweet moments the old magic took hold, potent as ever—until he remembered himself and what she'd done.

He tore his mouth away then and said, "Stop acting as if you're going to die," and if she'd dared, she'd have looked up to see if the thread of amusement she thought she might have heard in his voice was reflected in his eyes.

"Aren't we?" she quavered.

"No," he said, poking his head out from under the

table. "The worst is over and even if it weren't, you're not getting off that easily."

A minute later, it was all over—their brief moment of intimacy, the howling, screaming wind—and nothing to show for either but the rain pounding on the roof, thunder rumbling menacingly and lightning streaking across the lake. Miraculously, the pine tree was still standing and so was the cottage, though how defied explanation.

"You can come out now," Pierce said, wriggling away from her and going to inspect the damage. Rainwater driven through the open windows ran in channels along the old pine floor and dripped through the cracks between the ceiling beams.

"How can I help?" she asked, coming to stand beside him.

"There are towels upstairs on the shelf behind the bathroom door," he said. "Throw half of them down here to me, and use the rest to start mopping up in the bedroom."

The task kept them occupied for a further half hour, but finally the worst of the mess was cleaned up, the windows securely latched against another outburst, and there was nothing to distract either of them. They stood at opposite ends of the living room, staring at each other as warily as strangers stranded in a train station. Nicole thought that she'd rather have faced another tornado than the wild emotions churning the atmosphere.

Finally, he moved, shrugging his shoulders as though doing so would rid him of the irritation of her company. "I guess," he said, going to a cabinet beside the fireplace and extracting a bottle of red wine, "we might as well make this as painless as possible. Would you like me to light a fire? The air's a lot cooler in the wake of the tornado."

"Aren't we heading back to town?"

"In this storm?" The look he bent her way suggested only a moron would contemplate such a move. "Apart from the trees likely to come down, the road is probably flooded in a dozen places and quite impassable.''

As if to press home his point, a clap of thunder split the sky directly over the house, followed almost immediately by a brilliant flash of lightning and the distant sound of breaking glass.

''Sounds as if the place next door took a direct hit,'' he observed. ''Better line up some candles. We'll be needing them before long. You'll find a boxful in the top drawer of the small chest in the dining room.''

When she came back, he'd already set a match to the kindling in the hearth. ''I brought wineglasses, too,'' she said, and almost dropped the lot as another bellow of thunder ripped through the early night, and lightning arrowed over the sky, illuminating the lake.

He cast another dispassionate glance at her. ''It's only thunder,'' he said scornfully. ''It won't bite you.''

''And you wouldn't care if it did,'' she replied, stung again by his indifference.

''Not particularly,'' he said, filling the glasses and helping himself to one without bothering to offer her the other. ''I can't say your well-being is uppermost in my mind at the moment. I'm too busy trying to figure out how I'm going to explain to Tom that the woman he thought was only his nanny is really his aunt, but that she was too big a coward to let him know before now.''

''And then there's the matter of your own bruised ego to attend to,'' she couldn't help saying.

He glared at her. ''Exactly what is that supposed to mean?''

She snatched up the other glass and took a healthy swig. Not a very nice way to treat what was undoubtedly a very fine bottle of wine, but what did such niceties matter at a time like this? ''You're so busy nursing your injured feelings, Pierce,'' she accused, ''that you've never once considered mine.''

He almost spluttered into his glass. ''It doesn't strike me that—''

"For instance," she went on, undeterred, "do you have the faintest idea how I felt when I looked in the drawers in the bedroom upstairs and found clothes that had belonged to Arlene?"

"You had no business snooping in drawers," he shot back.

"No," she said. "I don't suppose I had, nor would I have dreamed of doing so if you hadn't mentioned that there were probably some of her things still here from the last time she visited. As it was, I couldn't help myself. All I could think was that she was probably the last person to touch those things until I came along."

A bubble of grief rose in her throat which she flushed away with another mouthful of wine. "I lifted out a sweater and smelled it—it held her scent, a trace of perfume, and there was a long blond hair caught in the button at the neck. And what struck me was that, although she's been dead nearly four months, that hair still shone with life and it was as close as I was ever going to come to touching her again."

"Stop it," he said.

"Then I looked in the closet and there was a pair of sandals on the floor that must have been hers. Her feet and mine were exactly the same size. Isn't that amazing? Those shoes fit me so perfectly that it was as if I'd worn them from the time they were new. And I thought, as I have so many times since I came to Morningside, that that was a discovery I should have been sharing with her. She was my sister, Pierce. My *sister*! And for most of her twenty-seven and a half years, I didn't know she existed. How would you have felt, if that had happened to you?"

"Like hell," he said, regarding her from hooded eyes. "But I wouldn't have made it an excuse to live a lie for the past however long it is since you sneaked your way into my house."

"How do you know? How can you say what you'd have done if you'd felt, as I did, caught up in a tragedy beyond human understanding and left with only a child to connect you to a part of your past—a child, I might add, entrusted to the care of a stranger who had no idea you even existed?''

''All you had to do was tell me.''

''And you'd have believed me?''

He swirled wine around in his mouth contemplatively, and swallowed. ''Naturally, I'd have asked to see the proof but if I'd been satisfied you were who you claimed to be, I'd have accepted you.''

She sat back in the chair across from his and watched him a moment. ''If that's so, then I did you a great injustice. But allow me to remind you that I'd suffered a terrible shock, that day I came to your house for the first time. I wasn't thinking clearly. The only thing I knew was that I needed to be near Tommy. I needed to be able to touch him, to hold him. To watch him sleeping, to know how his hair smelled after his bath, to listen to him breathing.''

She waved her hand, frustrated by her inability to put into words all that had prompted her to act as she had. ''I'm not saying this very well but if you'd ever suffered a loss, you'd know what I mean.''

''I have,'' he reminded her. ''I lost a cousin who was like a brother to me, in case you've forgotten. And you might like to think you're more closely related to Tommy than I am, but quite frankly, I don't see it that way. I've known him since he was born—not as well as I'd have liked, perhaps. The Navy doesn't take family occasions into too much account when it assigns a man to duty—but some connections run deeper than blood ties and mine to him is one of them.''

''Which is exactly what I was afraid you'd think if I'd admitted to who I was when I first met you. You'd have seen me as a threat and that was the last thing I wanted. But if you and Jim were as close as you say, you have to agree there's something about another person's physical presence that nothing else can quite equal.

You might have needed Tommy, but I needed him, too, to help me heal. And I truly believed I could help him to heal, too.''

"This is all very fine," Pierce said, in that flat, unemotional voice that chilled her despite the fire's leaping warmth, "but if you and Arlene were all set for such a grand reunion, how come she never mentioned it to me? We were practically next-door neighbors, after all, and it certainly wasn't the kind of news she needed to keep hidden.''

"We'd agreed to keep quiet about our relationship, at least for the first few days. We needed time alone together to get to know one another again before we let the rest of the world in on the secret. Jim knew that, and he agreed with us. I have letters to prove it—for the three months before I came out here, I corresponded and talked often on the phone with my sister. I even knew about you.''

His glance flickered over her. "So you were primed before you even got as far as my front door. No wonder you knew which buttons to push.''

"Oh, for heaven's sake, Pierce, stop looking for ulterior motives where none exist! I knew Jim had a relative who lived close by, and that was just about the extent of it. Believe it or not, we had more important things to talk about than such nitty-gritty details as your shoe size and favorite brand of toothpaste!''

He grimaced a little, as if he found that morsel of news somewhat indigestible. "I guess I deserved that.''

"I guess you did. And if you're disappointed in me for not being honest with you from the start, let me tell you I'm not exactly impressed with the way you're dealing with things now that they're out in the open. If you can't offer me forgiveness, the least you could do is show a little understanding. I made a mistake, but I'm not a criminal.''

He got up to add another chunk of wood to the fire, then straightened to his full height and arched his back, massaging the lower vertebra as he did so. "Are you hungry?"

How could he think about food at a time like this? "No," she said. "And even if I was, there's hardly anything left over from lunch."

"There'll be canned food, and probably stuff in the freezer, too. Arlene usually stocked up on supplies each spring when she and Jim came to open the cottage up after the winter." He collected the wine bottle and glasses, and jerked his head toward the kitchen. "Come and fill me in on more details while I rummage around."

Her heart gave a little lurch of hope at his invitation. Perhaps they were making some progress, after all. At least they were talking and if he didn't always say what she'd most like to hear, anything was preferable to his silence. "What else do you want to know?"

"How you found out about Arlene, how come you both ended up being adopted, why it took so long for the two of you to make contact again."

"You're asking for the story of my life."

"So?" He piled canned soup, crackers, coffee, powdered milk and frozen cannelloni on the kitchen counter. "It seems a fair exchange, wouldn't you say, considering all you know about me?"

"Why don't you just read the letters in the envelope?"

"I'd rather hear it from you," he said, topping up their wineglasses. "If you recall, from the day you applied for the job of nanny, I'm not particularly impressed with paper credentials. They might support a person's story, but they never give the whole picture. So start at the beginning, Nicole, and this time, don't leave anything out."

CHAPTER TEN

"YES, sir, Commander!"

Pierce paused in the act of unwrapping the plastic on the cannelloni and favored her with a sideways look loaded with warning. "Don't push your luck," he advised her quietly.

She shrugged, uncowed. She had no more shameful facts to reveal, so if he hoped to trick her into revealing any, he was in for a disappointment. "I grew up knowing I'd been adopted just before my fourth birthday because my natural father had abandoned my birth mother and she found she couldn't cope with single parenthood."

"That must have been tough to accept."

"No. My adoptive parents are wonderful. They fought hard to get me and never for a moment regretted the sacrifices they made. I adore them both. They gave me all the love and security any child could ask for."

"What sacrifices? Either they wanted to adopt a child or they didn't."

"They were in their mid-forties and considered too old to go through the usual channels, so they paid a private agency to find them a child they could take into their home and love."

"You mean, they bought you?"

"If you want to call it that, yes," she said, irked by his tone. "I prefer to think of it as their wanting me badly enough that they refused to let anything come between them and me."

"Much the same way that you didn't let anything come between you and Tom," Pierce said, thrusting the cannelloni into the oven as if he'd have liked to shove her in after it.

"I won't tolerate your insulting my family, Pierce," Nicole said flatly.

"No," he said after a pause, "nor should you. I apologize. But you say you didn't know you had a sister until recently and that strikes me as odd. I find it hard to believe a four-year-old would wake up one day and not notice that her family, as she knew it, had disappeared practically overnight. Tom certainly remembers his mother and father, as we both know to our cost."

"I had some fragmented memories, yes," Nicole acknowledged, perching on a tall stool and sipping her wine. "I remember a woman whom I presume was my birth mother, but I don't remember the color of her eyes, how tall she was, or whether she was fat or thin. But I vaguely recall her voice—worried and high-pitched— and retain a blurry sort of image of her standing at a kitchen table and pushing her hair away from her face. And I remember waking up in a small, dark room, and the sound of someone crying in the night."

"Arlene?"

"Or our mother. She was only sixteen when I was born—not much more than a child herself."

"You never heard from her again."

"Not a word, until last August." Slipping down from the stool, Nicole went to the table in the dining room and extracted the familiar worn envelope from the clutter of other papers scattered over the surface just as Louise had left them. "On my twenty-ninth birthday, my parents gave me a large sealed package which contained all the details of my adoption. They thought I should have it so that I could look through everything if and when I felt ready to do so. They'd debated leaving it for me in their estate but decided they wanted to give it to me while they were still alive, in case I had questions which only they could answer."

All the time she'd been talking, Pierce had been working around the kitchen, putting together a makeshift meal which smelled surprisingly good. But when she lapsed into silence, he turned from stirring a pot of soup and noticed her standing in the doorway, the small dog-eared envelope in her hand.

"Well? What did you find?"

"Mostly lawyer's records of the adoptive process, and copies of the reports written by the social workers who assessed my parents' suitability to take on a child. But also these."

She tipped two items from the envelope and laid them on the kitchen counter. "This," she said, smoothing out the creases from the sheet of lined paper torn from an old exercise book, "is a letter written by my birth mother, one of the two things I have left of her. The other..." She touched the faded old snapshot lovingly. "...is this picture of two little girls holding hands and standing side by side in long grass in a sunny garden."

As though unwilling to admit to any curiosity, Pierce hesitated a moment before putting down the spoon and coming to stand beside her, though not so close that he had to touch her. "May I see?"

She shrugged assent, and he picked up the photo. He looked at it intently, focusing first on the children, one blond, one dark, then shifting his attention to the shabby house in the background, and the porch which sagged at one end, and the washing hanging from a clothesline. Finally, he turned it over and read the inscription on the back: *Nicole and Arlene. South Dakota, July.*

Then he looked at Nicole again, and for the first time she saw a glimmer of sympathy in his blue eyes. "She didn't have much, did she?"

"No. And what she did have, she gave away. Would you like to read the letter?"

"I—" He raised his hand as if to touch her after all, perhaps to stroke her hair or offer some other gesture of comfort, then changed his mind and went back to stirring the soup. "I'm busy. You read it to me."

"All right." She picked up the sad, hopeless message which she knew by heart, right down to its bad spelling and misused punctuation. "There's no salutation or date. It just begins, *'I am giving my babies away because they'll never amount to anything if they stay in this hell-hole of a town, I'm 20 and my husband, has run off with another woman, I have'nt got no money nor education and I am tired of people felling sorry for me and leaving care packuges on my back porch as if there afraid I won't feed my babies right. Or something. I am going away to start out fresh where nobody knows me. Even though I love them, I know my little girls will be better off without me and the socail worker is sure they'll be put in good homes. Signed, Susan Mary Little.'"*

When she'd finished, Nicole raised her eyes and looked at Pierce. He stood transfixed at the stove, his expression shaken. "Oh, brother!" he muttered.

"Or sister," she said, turning away from his pity. "I won't bore you with an account of my emotions at reading this for the first time. Suffice it to say I was over-whelmed to realize that, somewhere, I had a sister. We were siblings who had grown into women without knowing each other. We had lost twenty-five years of being friends, of sharing each other's joys and heartaches. And I made up my mind that I wouldn't let another year go by without finding her."

"How did your parents feel about that?"

"They had no idea about my birth mother's letter and were as shocked as I was. They understood completely and offered to do everything they could to help me. It grieved them terribly to think of two such young children being separated, especially since they would gladly have taken both of us, had they known. But as I eventually discovered, Arlene was quickly adopted by a couple who, like most, wanted someone younger than a four-year-old, who often comes with too much history and too many problems. I was the difficult one to place which is why my parents were able to get me, despite their age.''

"It's a funny thing, but Arlene never mentioned her adoptive parents much,'' Pierce said. "They didn't even bother to come out for the funeral and they show no interest at all in Tom.''

"She wasn't close to them and I can understand why. When I went to see them, they flatly refused to help me find her. They claimed she'd always been a difficult child, never properly grateful for their having taken her in when her own mother had, as they so charmingly put it, 'dumped her.' They seemed very bitter that she'd chosen to marry and move to Oregon. They thought she should have stayed to look after them in their old age. The way they saw it, that was the only reason to have children in the first place.''

"Good God, no wonder she hadn't much use for them! In light of their attitude, how did you manage to track her down?''

"Through a private investigator. The trail led straight to her door and when I wrote to tell her about me—about us, she was as thrilled as I was.'' Nicole blinked and stared out of the window at the lightning still forking the sky. This part of the story never got any easier. "When I learned that she had a son who turned four in May—the same age I was when she and I were separated—it was as if, despite our separation, fate or God or however you want to describe it, had taken a hand in coordinating our lives so that we wouldn't feel like total strangers when we finally met again.

"In my case, what made everything even more special was the comfort it gave my parents to know that, when they died, I wouldn't be left completely alone. They encouraged me to take a leave of absence from the Clinic and spend as much time as possible getting to know my other family.''

Pierce topped up his wine again and asked, "How do they feel about the scam you pulled on me?''

Realizing nothing she'd said had persuaded him to forgive her, Nicole suppressed a sigh. "They were worried. Their advice was to tell you the truth immediately, if not sooner."

"Pity you didn't listen to them," he said.

"Yes. Hindsight is famous for its twenty-twenty vision, and if I had to do it all over again, I'd change things. But this is now."

"And unfortunately, you can't turn back time. The clock goes only one way."

"Exactly. Life goes on and I've had nearly three months to adjust. The anger isn't as acute and the sadness...well, it gets easier to bear. I'm able to think more clearly about it all now. But the day I knocked on Arlene's front door and found strangers packing away her things was different. I had no premonition of tragedy and was totally unprepared to deal rationally with it."

Another flash of sympathy darkened his eyes. "Exactly how did you find out?"

"When I asked for Mrs. Warner, the woman who answered the door told me I had the wrong address. 'You mean Commander Warner,' she said. 'He's the one who'll interview you but he's at the other house. We're just here to close this place up.'

"'Close the place up?' I said, fumbling to put the pieces back where they belonged and where they'd been for the last seven or eight weeks.

"'Well, yes,' she said. 'There's no point in keeping it open. The child, poor little mite, has gone to live with his uncle and the movers will be here first thing in the morning. I daresay the Realtor's sign will go up as soon as they're done, and I expect the place will sell quickly. Waterfront properties are scarce around here and very desirable.'

"'Uncle?' I said, clinging to that word, still hoping it meant that I'd come to the wrong house after all. Because the rest of what she'd said had nothing to do with my reason for being there. And that's when I learned that Arlene and Jim were dead and that you'd been named Tommy's legal guardian. I hadn't suspected a thing before then because Arlene had told me, the last time we spoke before I left home, that she and Jim were going to California to a wedding the week before I was due to get here.''

''Tom was supposed to go with them but they decided at the last minute to leave him with me and Janet. Hell!'' Pierce slammed the spoon on the stove and glared at her. ''If you'd had the guts to tell me the truth at the outset, we could have helped each other get through that terrible time.''

''Well, I didn't have the guts. All I knew, was that you were a bachelor but probably wouldn't remain one for long and that, in the meantime, you needed help looking after Tommy. I was desperate, shocked, bereaved, frightened. Then I met Louise and realized she was the lady in your life and that when you married her, you wouldn't need a nanny. So I buried any doubts I had about what I was doing and grabbed at the only chance I could see of forging a connection between me and Tommy, foolishly believing that if I established myself in your eyes as a decent, compassionate woman, you'd find it easier to accept my assuming a more permanent role in his life after you married.''

''So when did your plan change, Nicole?''

''Change?''

He filled two bowls with tomato soup. ''When did you realize it would suit your purposes much better if you became Mrs. Pierce Warner?''

''Is that what you think this is all about?'' she asked incredulously.

''You have to admit, it all hangs together. You supplant Louise, step in as my wife and thereby become Tom's stepmother. That way, you get everything you wanted, and then some.''

For a moment, she stared at him, stunned, then whispered, ''You stupid, arrogant bastard!''

"Gee, thanks," he said, unperturbed. "Talk about how to win friends and influence people!"

"If you truly believe I could be that conniving, I don't want you as a friend and I surely don't care to have you as a husband. For your information, I had a life before I met you and somehow I'll have one again. And being Tommy's aunt will be part of that life."

He pinioned her in a gaze as bleak as Siberia. "Are you threatening me, Nicole?"

She did not know this man with the iron-hard features. He was not the man who'd made love to her with such passion and tenderness. He was not the man who'd won her heart for the way he'd taken on the role of instant father without hesitation or a moment's real resentment. "No," she said sadly. "I'd never do that. But I'm appealing to you, please, not to cut me out of Tommy's life just because you've decided I'm no longer the person you want to have around for the rest of yours. If you'll allow me this one thing, Pierce, I'll never ask anything more of you, ever again."

He didn't answer. He compressed his lips and stared at a spot on the wall behind her, then carried the soup bowls into the dining room and set them at one end of the table.

When she didn't follow, he deigned to speak, tossing the question over his shoulder indifferently. "Aren't you going to eat?"

The mere thought made her ill. She felt raw inside, bleeding invisibly from a hurt so vicious, it left her reeling. "No," she said. "If it's all the same to you, I think I'll try to get some sleep."

"Suit yourself," he said in the same cold, unfeeling tone. "Take your pick of which bed you prefer."

That morning, she could have chosen from four. But when she went up to the room she'd used earlier, she found both beds in there soaked from the rain which had been driven in when the wind blew open the window.

Well, what the heck! Fully clothed, she climbed

aboard one of those in the second room, pulled the quilt over her legs and turned her back to the door. Not that she expected to get a wink of sleep, but at least feigning it would preclude the need for further conversation, should Pierce decide to join her.

What was the point of talking, after all? Despite an occasional softening in his attitude, nothing she'd said had changed his mind. It shouldn't have surprised her. She'd known from the start that he expected of others the same unbending code of ethics he demanded of himself.

Outside the rain had stopped and in the still aftermath of the tornado, a full moon rose above the trees. But thunder continued to snarl in the distance and branches of lightning still split the sky over the lake. She smothered a sigh. It was going to be a long, pain-filled night made none the easier for knowing that although she was alone with Pierce in this small, isolated cottage, they might as well have been continents apart.

Around midnight he came upstairs, the candle flame throwing his flickering shadow across the wall at the foot of the bed, attesting to the fact that the storm had indeed brought down power lines somewhere in the area.

He paused at the threshold of the room where she lay and she knew, from the way his shadow vanished as he backed out and went to the other room, that he was trying to avoid being near her. A moment later he was back, no doubt having discovered what she already knew about the soggy state of the beds next door.

Her back to him, she lay rigid as stone beneath the quilt, fighting to maintain an even breathing pattern as he set the candle on the floor, a move which projected his shadow half over the ceiling and down the top of the wall above the window.

She squeezed her eyes shut. She didn't want to see him undressing; it was too bittersweet a reminder of the intimacies they'd shared earlier. But she heard the rasp of a zipper opening, the rustle of fabric sliding down hair-roughened limbs, and then the creak of the old iron bedstead next to hers. When she opened her eyes again, the room was dark except for the pale gleam of moonlight sliding between the trees.

There was perhaps a foot of space separating his mattress from hers, with only a small pine cabinet standing between. Either of them could have reached out a hand to the other, a simple touch that said, "I'm sorry," or "Be patient. I'm trying to understand," or most of all, "I love you," without a word having to be spoken.

Yet neither of them did. They lay there, each wrapped up in their separate, lonely misery. Somehow, it was that more than anything else that had transpired between them that laid bare the utter devastation to their happiness.

The hours ticked by, marked by the diminishing growl of the storm as it made its way slowly eastward. Pierce turned once or twice, rustling the covers as he did so. His breathing was that of a man asleep, deep and even.

How would he react, Nicole wondered, if she were to crawl into bed beside him and he awoke to find her pressed against him, with her arms holding him fast to her? Would his body betray him before he could draw away from her? Would that be enough to mend what was broken between them?

Smothering a sigh, she stared out at the moon. She'd made enough mistakes. She wasn't about to add to the list by bartering her body for his favors. Sex couldn't restore love; it took trust to do that and she wasn't sure either of them could ever trust the other anymore.

She was sleeping when he crept from the room just after six the next morning. He didn't look at her; he didn't dare. It was safer not to let temptation get a foothold.

He had the car all packed and coffee made when she came downstairs. Unreasonably, the fact that she looked just as desirable with shadows under her eyes while he, with a day's growth of beard stubbling his chin and his hair standing on end, looked and felt like something a dog had just dug up, ticked him off royally. That the morning was as fresh and sunny as a daisy merely added insult to his sense of injury.

"I'd like to head back as soon as possible," he said, knowing he sounded short but unable to moderate his tone.

The fact remained that no matter how she tried to mitigate her behavior, she'd had any number of chances to tell him the truth, but she'd waited until she had him exactly where she wanted him before she'd been forthcoming. And who was to say he might not still be in the dark, if Louise hadn't gone snooping through her things?

The whole business amounted to more than broken trust. He'd lost a dream, a hope so fragile and new it couldn't easily bear too close a scrutiny. For the first time in his life, he'd seen himself with a woman he'd want through eternity, only to discover she wasn't at all what he'd made her out to be. She was an illusion, alluring and lovely on the outside to be sure, but underneath lay a cunning so perfectly clothed in womanly guile that he had not for a moment questioned his perceptions of her.

He scowled at the sun glinting off the kitchen window. He felt a real kinship with those men he'd know under his command whose relationships had gone sour when their backs were turned. Women were trouble, far more trouble than they were worth.

"I'm ready," she said from the dining room.

"Don't you want coffee?"

"No, thanks."

He shot a glance at her from beneath lowered lashes. Tote slung over her arm, she stood by the door, her expression remote and, damn it, unrepentant. As if her not having been able to sway him with her excuses and explanations the night before somehow had made him the transgressor and her the injured party.

She had a lot of chutzpah—too damned much!

"I've decided," he announced, when they'd navigated the mud-filled ruts of the country road and were speeding west on the main route back to the coast, "to take Tom to Arizona to visit his grandparents."

"Jim's family, you mean?"

"Uh-huh. My aunt is crippled with arthritis and the trip up here is too much for her, but I know both she and my uncle are anxious to spend some time with their grandson."

"When will you leave?"

"Next week. It'll take me that long to square things away at the office."

"How long will you be gone?"

"I'm not sure—six, eight weeks, maybe longer. I'll probably roll in a few long overdue business trips while I'm at it."

He ignored her sucked-in breath of dismay. He needed to put time and distance between them, to sort out his feelings. It was one thing to tell himself whatever they'd had was over, and another to believe it. The truth was, he didn't know how he felt.

"I'll miss Tommy," she said.

But not you. Now that I've blown my cover, I've got no further use for you. She didn't say as much; she didn't have to. The way she huddled as far away from him as she could get spoke for her.

"I daresay he'll miss you at first, but he'll have his grandparents to keep him occupied, and a child soon adjusts. You haven't played that big a part in his life for very long, after all."

The last was a low blow; pure retaliation and he knew it. But she took it without flinching, saying only, "In that case, I think I'll go home for a visit, too. My parents have been very worried about the...situation out here. They'll be glad to see I've survived it relatively unscathed."

"Yeah, well." Ticked off again that she seemed so able to pick up the pieces and get on with her life regardless of what he did with his, he steered too quickly into a hairpin bend. "I'll explain to Tom."

"I'll do my own explaining, thanks," she said coolly. "It's the very least I can do. It's not as if there's any point in my hanging around your house when he's not there to be looked after."

"No point at all," he replied, clenching his teeth.

"It'll probably be easier for Janet if I take Peaches, too."

"Probably."

"You have my parents' address and know where to find me, so I'll wait to hear from you when you get back."

"Do that," he practically snarled.

And just like that, it was over. He spent the following days clearing his office calendar and setting up tentative dates to visit various naval bases around the country. In addition to what she usually did with Tom, Nicole obviously spelled out the new plans in some way that the boy found acceptable because he was fired up all week about flying on a jet to see his grandparents.

"I put everything in my backpack," he informed Pierce, the night before they left. "Nicole helped me. I got all my shorts and my Duplo blocks and my pictures of Mommy and Daddy."

She sort of choked on her food at that.

"Good work, Tom," Pierce said, stifling the twinge of conscience her distress gave rise to. "We'll be off first thing in the morning."

"And I made a drawing for Grandpa."

"What about Grandma?"

"She prefers a card," Tom said, in that laughably grown-up way he had of saying things occasionally. "I'll make her a card on the jet."

"Sounds like a fine plan," Pierce said, and pretended not to notice the single tear rolling down her cheek.

· She didn't come down again after she'd put Tom to bed that night. He waited an hour or so, pacing up and down in the library, stopping every once in a while to stare out to sea, and wondering how in hell they'd managed to make such a screw-up of things.

Eventually, he decided twisting in the wind didn't agree with him, so he went up to find her. Her door was closed but he could hear her moving about inside. He knocked, and it took her a moment or two to answer.

When she did, he saw at once that she'd been crying. Probably sobbing, to be more accurate, because she gave one of those involuntary little hiccups that seemed to follow a real bout of female tears.

He didn't like the jolt that gave him. It seemed a sign of weakness. "I guess we should talk," he said, for want of a more original opening.

She pulled the door wider in mute invitation and when he stepped into the room, he saw that her suitcases were spread open on the floor and half stuffed with clothing. "You're heading out tomorrow, too?"

"Yes." She tore a tissue out of a box on the desk and blew her nose.

"What did you tell Tom?"

"That he was going on a plane to see his relatives, but because I had my car here, I was driving back to see mine."

"Did you tell him you're his aunt?"

"No," she said. "I thought he had enough to deal with and that you'd probably prefer to do that yourself."

"You sound just like him," he said, his throat aching suddenly. "The way you say 'prefer.'"

"Don't forget to pack his dee-dee before you leave. He never goes to bed without it."

He nodded. "I'll remember."

"And his vitamins. They're on the top shelf of the refrigerator door. And you'll need extra clothes. I left them on the dresser next to his closet."

"I'll manage," he said. "Is there anything else?"

She looked at him across the width of the room, her big brown eyes all bruised with pain. "Please let me see

. once in a while, Pierce. And keep me posted on
how he's coping.''

"Sure.''

They were talking as if she wasn't coming back; as if
they really had reached the end of the road. He wished
he could tell her otherwise but the doubts and resentment
still simmered inside. "I'll let you know where we are,
how Tom's doing,'' he said.

She stared at her hands, which were clenched together.

"After you went to bed that night at the cottage, I
read through everything Louise had brought out. If it
makes any difference, there's no doubt at all in my mind
that you and Arlene were sisters and I want you to know
how sorry I am that you never got to know each other
again.''

"Thank you,'' she said, her voice thick with tears.

Pain sliced through him and he knew the easy fix
would be to take her in his arms, to kiss her. Just to take
her. But he was looking for more than a Band-Aid so-
lution and there was a wanting in him that went deeper
than sex, that left him feeling raw and empty inside. It
wasn't just her motives he had to come to terms with;
his own needed some examining, too.

"We'll work this out,'' he said. "I just need time—
to figure out in my own mind...''

"Yes,'' she said politely. "Of course.''

Still, he wanted her. His flesh yearned for her.

"Well,'' he said, extending his right hand as he would
to another man, "drive safely.''

"Mm-hmm.''

If she'd started wailing then, he could probably have
walked away. It was her courage that defeated him; that
and the smallness of her hand in his. "Oh, hell,'' he
groaned, and before he knew it, was kissing her, im-
printing the taste and texture of her on his body and soul.
Grabbing a handful of her hair and weaving his fingers
through it as if it were a lifeline to sanity, a passport to
happiness.

Her mouth felt like flowers, her skin tasted of salt, a marriage of land and sea. Shudders of emotion rippled through her, light as a morning breeze filling a sail, and he knew he had to leave her then, before he drowned in the need she awoke in him.

"I'll be in touch," he said hoarsely.

"I'll be waiting," she said.

CHAPTER ELEVEN

AUTUMN in Wisconsin usually offered its residents grim warning of the winter ahead. That year, however, was an exception. Though the nights were long and touched with frost, memories of Indian summer still gilded the days.

During the time it took for summer to slide into fall, she began the slow process of healing. In walking Peaches by the shores of Lake Mendota and training her to come to heel, to sit, to stay, Nicole reclaimed some of the tranquillity of the old days—the Days Before, as she came to think of them.

In some small measure, she recaptured the simple pleasure of a quiet evening with her parents; the feel of leaves crunching underfoot on a cool morning, the fragrance of her mother's kitchen as the dinner hour approached. Her thirtieth birthday came and went.

And then in September, everything came crashing down again when she realized she was pregnant.

"Good Lord, that man has a lot to answer for!" her father exploded, when he heard.

"Calm down, Dan. It takes two," her mother reminded him.

But Nicole held herself entirely to blame. A woman of her educational background had no excuse for being so careless. Yet she couldn't bring herself to regret her pregnancy. Wanting children, a man of her own to love, were as much a part of her as her solid, Midwestern upbringing. That she should find both at such cost was too cruel.

"Tell Pierce, honey," her mother urged. "He has a right to know, and every child deserves two parents."

"He's got more than rights," her father fumed. "He's got obligations to our daughter."

Nicole didn't want Pierce's obligations; she wanted *him*, but only if he came to her of his own accord, without reservation. He'd left her because he felt she'd ambushed him with deceit. Would he view finding himself being lassoed into fatherhood as anything less than another attempt at entrapment on her part? And if he did, was it selfish of her to want this baby anyway?

Damn it, no! She'd been robbed once; she would not let herself be robbed again.

"You've got another postcard from Tommy," her father said, riffling through the mail during breakfast, one morning in November. "And a letter."

From Pierce. Although neither of them mentioned his name unless she did, she knew from her parents' sudden air of expectation that they both waited, watching her face, hoping to see it flood with happiness as she read his latest news.

"They're in North Carolina," she said, picking up Tommy's card. "The naval base at Charlottestown. Tommy visited the bridge of a destroyer. And he wrote his own name at the bottom here, see?"

"When's that man going to get tired of trying to hang on to his illustrious past and start dealing with the present?" her father grumbled. "Living out of a suitcase is no sort of life for a four-year-old boy."

"They're combining pleasure with a lot of business." It was the same excuse she'd been giving all along.

"And where does that leave you?" her father wanted to know.

She tapped the latest letter against the edge of the table, afraid of what it might contain. She knew to the last mile the number of cities Pierce and Tommy had visited, the far-flung relatives her nephew had met, the sights he'd seen. But she hadn't the faintest inkling of where, if anywhere, her relationship with his uncle was headed.

In mid-October, Pierce had written to suggest she join him and Tommy at Disneyland for a couple of days. But her morning sickness had still been so severe, she'd been afraid she wouldn't be able to hide it. In retrospect, though, turning down Pierce's invitation didn't seem such a smart decision. He hadn't issued another and she wasn't sure he ever would. Unless this latest letter…?

Swallowing, she pushed aside her waffles. Just the sight of his handwriting was enough to put her stomach in an uproar. Slitting open the envelope, she withdrew the single sheet of paper inside. She read it twice and felt a warmth flow through her.

"Everything okay?" Her parents sat on the edge of their chairs, watching her as if she were a chick just hatching from the egg.

"He wants to know if I'd like Tommy to spend Thanksgiving here before they head home for Christmas."

"I can see you hate the idea," her father observed dryly. "When's the little guy coming?"

"Next Wednesday, unless Pierce hears differently from me. He's booked Tommy on a flight that gets in just after three."

Suddenly, it wasn't so hard to take pleasure in the approaching holiday season. Suddenly there was a reason to shop and plan, to make lists and fuss over menus that would appeal to a little boy. Suddenly, there wasn't so much time in which to dwell on her own problems, to wonder if Pierce thought about her as often as she thought about him.

The next five days passed in a dizzying round of preparations. She and her mother baked, her father rooted around in the attic and found the wooden train set he'd bought over thirty Christmases ago for the son he'd never had. And like all the other residents of Maple Bluff, he strung their house and garden with Christmas lights, threading them along the eaves and through the branches of the tree outside the front door.

The weather changed the night before Tommy's arrival, a near-blizzard that swept down from Canada with little prior warning. A bad omen, Nicole thought. Would he have forgotten her? Be homesick for Pierce and the mild west coast winter he was used to?

Her parents had planned to go with her to meet him at the airport. "Better take the four-wheel-drive," her father decided, after checking the local forecast. "We'll never make it otherwise."

The roads were a mess, with blowing snow over black ice. Abandoned cars huddled in clumps along the highway, sometimes locked together in a frozen embrace.

A sliver of fear stabbed the length of Nicole's spine. What if the runway—if Tommy's plane...?

No! Resolutely, she aborted that particular avenue of thought. There had been enough tragedy, enough grief. It was Thanksgiving, a time to give thanks for what was, to let go of what was not nor ever would be. Arlene and Jim were gone and perhaps it was time to reconcile herself to the fact that, in a different way, so was Pierce.

His travels had taken him to naval bases in Alameda and San Diego and Long Beach, California; to Kingsbay, Georgia, and Pensacola, Florida, and Norfolk, Virginia. The weeks had spun by, stretching summer into late fall. But for all that he'd kept in touch by mail, he hadn't cared enough about her to find time to visit Madison, Wisconsin.

Tommy's flight was thirty minutes late arriving. It was the longest half hour of Nicole's life. In the last six months she'd become intimate with fear and it had lingered, obstinate as a low-grade infection. Content most of the time to prowl softly at the back of her mind, it flared up every once in a while to remind her that happiness could be snatched away without a moment's notice.

As those thirty minutes ticked by, it took hold with a savagery that left her numb with apprehension. Her parents were at her side. All around, people were full of the holiday spirit, greeting each other with hugs and laughter. But she stood alone, isolated in a dread as intense as it was irrational.

"He's landed." Her father touched her shoulder lovingly, a gesture intended to comfort but which instead made her cry. "The announcement just went up on the monitor."

Her mother squeezed her arm. "You can relax, honey."

"It's hormones," she whimpered pathetically. "You know I'm not usually like this."

"You were worried. He's such a little boy to be traveling alone, especially in this weather."

She mopped at her eyes with a tissue. "Do you think he'll recognize me, Mom?"

"Of course he will. In no time at all, it'll be as if you'd never been apart. And when he sees Peaches and how much she's grown..."

"Here they come," her father said, indicating the passengers trickling through double doors on the far side of the baggage carousel. "You won't have to wait much longer."

"He'll be one of the last to deplane," Nicole said. "He'll have to wait for a flight attendant to bring him out."

Still, she scanned the crowd anxiously. What if he'd missed the plane, or Pierce had changed his mind?

She turned to her mother, one woman to another communicating without need for words. "He'll be here," her mother said, understanding.

And suddenly he was, coming up behind her and saying, "Hi, Nicole!" while she was staring out at the thickly falling snow and praying that nothing would happen to spoil this day. She spun around to find him smiling up at her, a little taller than when last she'd seen him but as adorable as ever.

Dropping down, she held out her arms. He flung himself at her and wound his own so tightly around her neck that she almost choked. It was the most wonderful sensation in the world. "I buyed you a Christmas present," he piped excitedly, "but I can't tell you what it is because it's a surprise."

"You're my Christmas present," she told him, her voice choked with emotion, "and all the surprise I need."

A pair of men's black leather boots appeared in her line of vision, topped by a pair of legs covered in dark gray cords. "I'm sorry to hear that, Nicole. I was hoping you could stand one more."

His voice seemed to come from a very great distance. It took forever for her glance to travel the length of those legs and up past the hip-length suede jacket to the broad shoulders. And even longer before she dared bring herself to meet that familiar, level blue stare.

"Pierce?" She barely breathed his name in case she broke the spell and he disappeared.

"Has it been so long that you barely recognize me?" he said.

It had been an eternity. It had been a nightmare. And now she was surely dreaming. Because his eyes were caressing her, his voice was wooing her.

But the hand he held out to draw her to her feet was warm and sure, a composite of all-too-real flesh and bone. The arm he slid around her waist was firmly muscled beneath the fleece-lined suede.

Her waist! Just the week before, she'd shopped for looser clothing to tide her over until she was ready to advertise her condition to the rest of the world with full-blown maternity wear. Yet here was Pierce, literally dropping down out of the sky to land at her feet and learn the fact firsthand before she had a chance to prepare either herself or him for the disclosure.

"Ahh!" Hearing her own gasp of dismay and seeing the same emotion reflected in his eyes as she backed away, she conjured up a feeble smile. "Pierce," she said again, wrapping her coat firmly across her middle and hugging it there with both hands, "I wasn't...expecting you."

Expecting? Oh, for crying out loud, Nicole, if he wasn't suspicious before, he should be now!

His expression went beyond suspicious to outright thunderstruck. "No," he said, his eyes widening as confusion faded into comprehension. "I know. I wasn't...expecting, either." He gestured ambiguously in the region of her midriff and she thought she had never before seen him at such a loss, not even when he learned she'd been lying to him for months. "It seems we have more to talk about than I realized." The way his glance darted to her midriff again made her feel big as a house. He cleared his throat. "Quite a...bit more."

Immediately behind him, her parents hovered, clearly uncertain of their role in this unexpected turn of events but too caught up in the drama of the moment to put themselves at a discreet distance. "This is Pierce," she informed them unnecessarily.

He noticed them then. In particular he noticed her father's steely observation, and squared his shoulders.

"My mother and father," she said. "Dan and Nancy Bennett."

"I'm delighted to meet you, Mrs. Bennett." He shook her mother's hand and gave her a brief, charming smile before turning to face her father. It occurred to Nicole that they looked like two aggressive dogs about to settle territorial dominance.

"How do you do, sir?"

"About as well as you might expect, given my daughter's—"

"Precisely." Pierce stood four inches taller than her father, an advantage he had no hesitation in exploiting. Dan Bennett was a successful businessman by anyone's standards but he wasn't a match for Pierce Warner in Commander mode.

"And this is Tommy." Anxious to defuse the moment, Nicole urged the child forward.

"Hi," he said, and tugged at her mother's hand. "I have to go wee-wee."

As a tension breaker, it was heaven-sent. By the time Nicole and her mother had found a washroom and taken care of Tommy's most pressing need, Pierce had collected the luggage and her father had the car waiting at the entrance.

Once settled in the back seat with Tommy between them, Pierce trapped Nicole in another level glance. "We need some time alone."

"Yes," she said.

"Soon."

"I'll try to arrange it."

"Make sure you do."

Well, some things certainly never changed, she thought, folding her hands over her waist. "Yes, Commander," she said.

A baby! His!

Well, so much for taking a person by surprise!

He'd thought he'd have the upper hand, would catch Nicole unawares and sweep her off her feet before she had the chance to take his belated apologies and give them the deep six, but she'd completely outmaneuvered him before he'd had the chance to utter much more than a word.

Pregnant! About four months along as far as he could determine. Not that he had any previous experience to fall back on in these matters, but he could count. And by his reckoning, it had been exactly fifteen and a half weeks since he'd first made love to her and thirteen weeks, two days and eight hours since the last time. They had been the most miserable thirteen weeks, two days and eight hours of his entire life.

He stood before the fireplace in the living room of the Bennetts' elegant home, and watched the flames curling around the logs in the hearth. Nicole had promised to join him there as soon as Tom fell asleep and her parents, taking the broad hints he'd dropped, had settled themselves in front of the TV in the family room on the other side of the kitchen.

Dinner had been tense, to put it mildly. Tommy was overtired and overexcited. Peaches, who'd grown to the size of a small pony, had misbehaved and been banished from the room for begging. And Dan Bennett...

Well, Dan Bennett wasn't impressed with the man who'd come to lay claim to his daughter. In his place, Pierce wouldn't have been, either. His actions of late had little to commend them.

But Nicole... He inhaled deeply, savoring the memory of how she'd looked when she'd suddenly found him standing beside her at the airport. She'd lit up inside, as if seeing him had brought her to life. Her skin had turned luminous. Her mouth had reminded him of dawn at sea, all soft and rosy. And her eyes—hell, he'd marveled at the Southern Cross, the Northern Lights, and just about every constellation in between, but none had equaled the glow in her eyes.

She'd worn an off-white winter coat with a big fur collar drawn up around her throat, and long black boots of glove-soft leather. She'd looked, he thought, like a Russian princess. Elegant, beautiful. And pregnant.

He had wanted to kneel down and kiss her feet. To beg her forgiveness for letting his stupid male pride keep them apart for so long. What a fool he'd been!

The door behind him opened. "Hi," she said. "Sorry I took so long."

"That's okay. Is Tom asleep?"

"Out like a light. It's been a long day for him."

And for me, Pierce thought. He'd been under the same roof with her for the last five hours and hadn't even kissed her yet.

"Why didn't you let me know?" he said, gesturing at the straight blue wool dress she wore which, despite its cut, couldn't didn't quite hide the slight swell of her pregnancy.

She tilted one shoulder in a shrug. "I wanted to wait."

"For what? Until your father had me lined up in his shotgun sights?"

She darted a glance at him and seemed relieved to see him smiling. "I was afraid you'd be upset."

"Sweetheart!" he said, drawing her toward him. "I'm not upset. If I'd known, I'd have been here sooner—"

"I didn't want that," she said, pulling back from him a little. "I didn't—I *don't* want you feeling coerced. We didn't part on the best of terms, Pierce. You felt I'd abused your faith in me, that you couldn't trust me and—"

"I was wrong," he said, ushering her to the couch and pulling her down onto his lap. "I was hurt to begin with, I admit. I tried not to love you. I went away and tried to hold on to my past because I thought what I used to have was better than anything I had in the present. But I was wrong. I want more than yesterday, I want today and tomorrow. I'm not a seaman anymore, Nicole, I'm a family man and glad of it. And I want a future with you. Have I left it too late to say I'm sorry?"

"No," she whispered. "I'm sorry, too, that I ever gave you reason to doubt me."

"Stop blaming yourself," he said, and wished he could have found the generosity of spirit to tell her that at the cottage, when she'd needed to hear it the most. He knew that, if the situation had been reversed, she wouldn't have judged him so harshly. "Now that I've managed to put aside my pride, I can see that, in your place, I might have acted as you did."

"No, you wouldn't," she said. "You've never flinched from the truth in your life."

"Yes, I have," he said, locking his arms around her. "I walked away from it the day I left you. If I'd dared to be honest with myself then, I'd have admitted it wasn't you I was afraid to trust, it was me. But I've learned you can't run away from feelings. They stick with you until you come to terms with them. The question is, did I take too long to come to my senses?"

She cupped his face in her hands and he saw that her eyes were full of tears. "No. I would have waited forever for you," she whispered brokenly. "And I promise you now, on my word of honor, that I'll never lie to you again or give you reason to question your faith in me."

He had not known a heart could feel so full. After all the weeks of hurting, he had not dreamt she could heal him so easily.

"Will you come back to Morningside with me, Nicole?" he asked hoarsely, and placed his hand on her abdomen. "Will you marry me and be a mother to Tommy, as well as to this baby? Will you let me love you and make you forget the unhappiness you've suffered this last year?"

"Yes," she said, covering his hand with hers.

She'd thought he'd never kiss her but at last he did, drawing her close in a fusion of heart and soul, as well as of body.

"I love you," he said, and they were the most magical, the most healing words in the world.

Nicole's loneliness melted in their warmth. Her grief softened. Of course, it could never be entirely forgotten but at last it slipped into the past where it belonged, and made way for the here and now.

"I love you, too," she said, drowning in the blue depths of his beautiful eyes. "I will love you forever."

HARLEQUIN PRESENTS®

How could any family be complete without a nineties nanny?

NANNY WANTED!

...as a friend, as a parent or even as a partner...

A compelling new series from our bestselling authors about nannies whose talents extend way beyond looking after the children:

**January 1998—THE SECRET MOTHER
by Lee Wilkinson (#1933)**

**February 1998—THE LOVE-CHILD
by Kathryn Ross (#1938)**

**March 1998—A NANNY NAMED NICK
by Miranda Lee (#1943)**

**April 1998—A NANNY IN THE FAMILY
by Catherine Spencer (#1950)**

P.S. Remember, nanny knows best when it comes to falling in love!

Available wherever Harlequin books are sold.

DEBBIE MACOMBER

invites you to the

HEART OF TEXAS

Join Debbie Macomber as she brings you the lives
and loves of the folks in the ranching community
of Promise, Texas.

If you loved Midnight Sons—don't miss
Heart of Texas! A brand-new six-book series
from Debbie Macomber.

Available in February 1998
at your favorite retail store.

Heart of Texas by Debbie Macomber

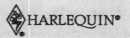
HARLEQUIN®

Catch more great

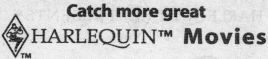

HARLEQUIN™ Movies

featured on the movie channel tmc

Premiering April 11th
Hard to Forget
based on the novel by bestselling
Harlequin Superromance® author
Evelyn A. Crowe

Don't miss next month's movie!
Premiering May 9th
The Awakening
starring Cynthia Geary and David Beecroft
based on the novel by Patricia Coughlin

If you are not currently a subscriber to
The Movie Channel, simply call your
local cable or satellite provider for more
details. Call today, and don't miss out
on the romance!

the movie channel tmc   HARLEQUIN™
Makes any time special.™

100% pure movies.
100% pure fun.